THE GAS STATION MOTEL

A JACKLYN STONE THRILLER

JACKLYN STONE THRILLERS
BOOK 5

SUSAN SPECHT ORAM

SOS COMMUNICATIONS LLC

THE GAS STATION MOTEL

A Jacklyn Stone Thriller

Susan Specht Oram

SOS Communications LLC

Published by SOS Communications LLC in 2026

www.susanspechtoram.com

First Edition

ISBN: 979-8-9937061-0-8 (ebook)

ISBN: 979-8-9937061-1-5 (paperback)

✿ Formatted with Vellum

PREVIOUSLY

PREVIOUSLY IN:

SHORE LODGE

Jacklyn Stone, a grieving widow and garden store owner, is admitted by her greedy son to Shore Lodge, a secure psychiatric facility. She must escape to rescue her dog and reclaim her home.

BY MIDNIGHT

Jacklyn helps friends gather money to keep a debt collector at bay, but the clock is ticking in a race against time.

THE WINTER STORM

Jacklyn and her friends return to Shore Lodge to free four residents from a secure psychiatric unit on Christmas

Eve. But a storm is brewing, and her devious son is out to thwart her every move.

THE COLD NIGHT

A snowstorm traps Jacklyn and her dinner party guests with her conniving son. When Jacklyn's friend's daughter is kidnapped, FBI agents must find the missing teenage girl.

AVALANCHE

Hearing intruders in her home, Jacklyn grabs a candlestick and charges toward danger, catching her bitter child in an unforgivable act. Her son ignores avalanche warnings, and his wilderness trek turns into a nightmare.

THESE LIES

An unscrupulous neighbor pretends to have cancer to get back at her ex-husband for leaving her. Jacklyn is pulled into her neighbors' drama, and she encounters new difficulties building her housing development.

1

———

EMILY

I close my suitcase, set the cat carrier on the bed and place a call to my last hope for help. My aunt Jacklyn answers, and I let out a little sigh. I don't want to move to her waterfront town in Washington State, but I have no choice. In a trembling voice, I say, "Hi, this is Emily. I'm leaving soon, and I'll be at your place tomorrow around two in the afternoon."

In an upbeat voice, she says, "I'm looking forward to seeing you and having you stay with me until you're settled. Enjoy the scenery and call if you're delayed, or you decide to stop along the way for an extra day."

I stare at the ceiling and frown. "I don't really have the money for that, and I want to get to your place. I appreciate you offering to letting me stay with you, but are you sure your dog will get along with my cat?"

Jacklyn says, "You've got enough on your plate with

picking up and moving, so put that out of your mind. Buddy likes cats, and if they don't get along, I'll keep him on a leash in the house. Don't worry about it."

"Okay, I'll see you tomorrow. Thanks."

We say goodbye, and I pick up the cat carrier and my suitcase. My tabby cat meows, and I head down the stairs of my best friend's house, where I've been staying while searching for a new job. I let the screen door slap closed behind me and make my way to the car.

Mellie, my best friend, follows me outside, buffing her nails. I get the feeling she's more than ready to say goodbye to her freeloading friend. I've been living in her guest bedroom for the last two months and not paying rent.

Gently placing my cat carrier in the front passenger seat, I set the suitcase in back. Tears trickle down my cheeks, and I wipe them away with the back of my hand. This wasn't supposed to happen. I tried to find work.

Mellie says, "That's all you're taking?"

I shrug. "I don't have much, as you know."

She tilts her head. "Too bad you got laid off, Blinks."

Hearing my childhood nickname, I fiddle with my tortoise shell glasses. I've lived in this town my whole life, but after I lost my job, I couldn't find a new one, so it's time to move on. By leaving, I'll escape the shame of being seen as a loser who can't afford to go out and have drinks and dinner with friends. But in truth, I don't have many friends. Mellie is practically the only person I socialize with, and her family is wealthy, so she doesn't understand my limited resources as an only child with no living parents and not much in my bank account.

My throat tightens with tears. "I'm scared about moving. I hope I'll find a job soon at a jewelry store in Millersville, like the one I had here."

She tips her head back and laughs. "Get over it and move on. Branch out and do something new for work. Don't stay stuck in the first job you got in high school. Broaden your horizons and think big."

I roll my eyes. She was the perky alpha player in our high school pack, and I'm a quiet introvert who keeps to herself. For years, Mellie has pushed me to strive for something better and go to college, like she did, but I was happy working in a cozy back room at the store, playing forties big band swing music on the radio at low volume, like the owner, Mr. Redburn, preferred. But when he died, his kids sold the store, and I lost my job six months ago. I'm tired of eating a scrambled egg with rice and carrot sticks for dinner. There has to be more to life than my lonely, meager existence.

My cat meows, and I say to Mellie, "I'd better get going, so I guess this is goodbye. If you need to find me, you know where I'll be staying tonight, at The Gas Station Motel."

A gentle breeze blows, and she smiles, pushing back strands of blond hair from her face. "Enjoy your stay there. I've heard it's a great place to stop overnight, so that's why I recommended it."

I cock my head, because it's strange for Mellie to know anything about an older motel in the middle of nowhere. From what I saw online, it's definitely not her style. But she's on social media a lot, so maybe she bumped into some credible information. She's smart, so I follow her advice most of the time.

She leans in and gives me a hug, patting my back, but it feels stiff and forced. Before I break down in tears for what I've lost, including proximity to the home I grew up in that was sold when my folks died, I climb in the car and close the door. Starting the car, I wave to her, but she stands with her hands on her hips, frowning and staring into the distance.

I bite my lower lip, feeling the final tugs from an undercurrent of jealously running between us. Now that I'll be gone, she'll have our hometown of Baker, Oregon all to herself. Mellie rules over others by laughing, flirting and spending her father's money. Meanwhile, I'll be in a new place scrambling again, probably going nowhere fast.

Driving away, I grip the wheel leaving my past behind and head toward an uncertain future. Seeds of doubt sprout in my mind about the room I booked for tonight at The Gas Station Motel. Mellie recommended it, but she's never stayed there, and photos online featured dated furniture, worn carpet and dim lighting. But it's the only available lodging in the area I'll be passing through, so I'll stick with my plan. At least one small detail in my life is nailed down.

I say to my cat Mint Julep, "I don't know how this will end up, but we'll hang in there and find a way to have fun. This is a huge change, and I'm glad you're with me on this journey."

The cat doesn't answer, and my stomach growls. I don't want to eat the peanut butter and honey sandwich I packed yet, because that's all I brought to consume, along with a bottle of water filled from Mellie's kitchen faucet.

Humming a tune, I drive past farm fields. If it doesn't work out at my aunt's, and I don't get a job in Millersville, I'll move on. I haven't picked out a final destination. Heading west, I have no idea where I'll end up, but it will be a place that speaks to my soul and tells me to stay. I'd like to end up living near the water, after being land-locked, so Millersville would work.

A thought skitters past, and I nod. Perhaps I could work as a boat cleaner and polish brass, chrome and fiber-glass. I bet they have people doing things like that in mari-nas. I say, "It's time for my luck to turn around."

Julep meows, and I say, "I hear you, and I feel that way too. I don't want to go, but we have no choice."

Hours later, I wrinkle my nose at the smell of cow manure wafting from a field. A million worries tumble through my mind, and I murmur, "We'll find our way, I hope."

But the only reply I get is from my stomach rumbling

regrets. I pull out a sandwich and bite down on sourdough bread slathered with peanut butter and honey. The sky is dark, and it's long past dinner time. I'll be late checking into the motel room, but I mentioned that when I made the reservation, so it won't be a problem.

A flicker of concern flits through my mind, and I wonder if Aunt Jacklyn's dog really does like cats, or if she was just saying that. Dogs chase cats. If I have to move out to protect Julep, I will, but I doubt I'll find a landlord who will accept pipe dreams for rent payments.

I turn on the radio, and my worries fade away. Everything will be fine. All I need to do is stay awake and drive, check into the motel and sleep. I'll be on my way the first thing in the morning.

I break into a wide smile and settle into my seat. Like Mom used to say, all will be well, and we'll have blue skies from now on. But a little bird of apprehension sits on my shoulder, chirping about my upcoming accommodations for the night. I've never stayed alone in a motel before, and I hope my cat and I will be safe. If anything happens, I'll use my phone to call for help.

A chill creeps up my spine, and I shiver, gripping the wheel tight. I hope I haven't made a mistake by stopping at a rundown motel in a remote area. The fact that my friend was singing the place's praises was suspicious. If I don't like the motel, I'll get in my car and find somewhere else.

Letting out a yawn, I swat the idea away. I'm too tired

to keep driving beyond the Gas Station Motel. I need to sleep. Minutes tick by, and I drum on the steering wheel, waiting for the motel to appear in the headlights.

Rolling down the driver's side window halfway, cold night air rushes in, whipping past my cheeks. I shiver and blink in the breeze, straightening my back and telling myself to stay awake.

"We'll be there soon, and it'll be fine, Mint Julep."

2

———

JACKLYN

My niece hangs up, and I pocket my phone. I haven't seen her in years, and I have no idea how the plan to be roommates will work, because the two of us are such different ages. My friend Mercury sits at the dining table poring over plans for my new project for tiny homes and a fenced dog park on a hill above town, with views looking west to the San Juan Islands.

I slide into a seat by him and say, "I sort of wish I hadn't extended that invitation. This girl might expect to stay in my home forever, because we're family. But I have the feeling she lacks get up and go. All she's done in life is work at a jewelry store in their back room. Where's her drive and ambition?"

Mercury cocks his head and smiles. "Not everyone has

your energy, dear. All I can say is, don't judge. Besides, she's young."

I purse my lips. "She's in her twenties, which might mean trouble for me. She might have parties and play loud music late at night, which I wouldn't like. I'm worried about how this'll work out."

He pats the table. "Don't get ahead of yourself and whip up a dark storm cloud before she arrives. I'm sure it'll be fine."

"I hope you're right. It's a risk, not having seen her in so many years, but she needs help."

Mercury nods. "Like your friend Irena, you want to help everyone. You both run to the rescue."

I cross my arms. "Which reminds me of Jenna and her situation down the block. I thought she handled her husband inviting his ex-wife to live in their house fine without much of my help. That must've been a trial. It's too bad Zoila weaseled her way out of jail. I wonder where she is now? She's probably aiming her sights on a new target somewhere else."

"That'd fit her style."

Shaking my head, I say, "I'm shocked about Jenna's husband. I never thought Kirk was the type to embezzle money from employers. He seemed normal and nice, until Zoila showed up. He blamed his behavior on Zoila's influence, but the judge didn't buy his story, so he's locked up in jail for a long time."

Mercury shifts in his seat. "Zoila seems to bring out the worst in people."

My hands form fists. "She has a knack for doing that. I was ready to throttle her with my bare hands, when she rubbed me the wrong way and wouldn't stop feeding the raccoons. But Jenna will be fine on her own, and she's keeping her house."

Mercury taps a blueprint. "Time to get back to work?"

I lean forward. "Yes, that's enough neighborhood gossip for now. I've been thinking about this new, revised project, and I'd like the dog park to be bigger, so people can make natural footpaths around the perimeter and other trails that will intersect in the middle, where we'll have the best view of the water."

He chuckles. "Is the most important part of the project for you the tiny homes or the dog park?"

I grin and lean down, rubbing my beagle-mix dog Buddy's soft ears. "The dog park, of course. When I was at Gigi's Café yesterday, a few people stopped to ask me about signing up for a tiny home, so there's interest, and that's good."

"Have you started a wait list?"

"Yes, I did."

He adjusts a red bow tie clipped to his long gray beard. "How are you feeling about not building the big, fancy homes in a subdivision? Any regrets?"

"Not yet. The scaled-down project will be easier to build than Albert's and Dusty's dream of big homes with tall staircases leading up to five bedrooms and huge bathrooms with soaking tubs and two-person showers. That was their dream, not mine, so out with the old and in with the new."

"That's good to hear."

I study the old site plan. "I can't have road construction within six-hundred-sixty-feet of the bald eagle nest on my property, so that put a wrench in the works. I suppose I could make it an open area with park benches."

"But it could attract the wrong crowd, by being out of the way. Your park could be a perfect place for people to go to sell drugs or do who knows what."

I scoff and wave a hand, brushing away his concerns. "People in town won't do that. We can trust them, now that's Zoila's gone, and Dusty is locked in Shore Lodge, and Kirk's in jail. People will appreciate the open space and help take care of it. Nothing will go wrong."

He raises his eyebrows. "If you say so." Buddy stretches and yawns. Mercury says, "It's time for his walk, isn't it? I swear, your dog can tell time."

I glance outside at winter rain coming down hard. "Might as well get it done. The forecast says it's going to rain all day with no sunbreaks. We'll come home and get warm and dry, drink more coffee and finish reviewing the plans."

I pull a rain jacket over my down vest and leash up my dog, but wonder if I was too cavalier when I rejected Mercury's cautious words. Graffiti and vandalism happens in the best of places. With a sigh, I decide to worry about it later, if and when I need to.

Heading outside, wind whooshes by, evergreen trees sway, and worries fly through my mind. My scaled-down plans will cost less money to build than a subdivision, but my bank account would benefit from a silent investor backing the project. I'll ask Irena if she wants to chip in, because I suspect she may have inherited her former boyfriend's investment accounts after he passed away. She might be eager to join my exciting new venture, and I'd welcome her energy and input.

Wiping rain from my eyes, we march along, and Buddy trots through puddles with a spring in his step. Rain peppers my face, and it's cold enough that I can see my breath.

I slip a hand through Mercury's arm, and we smile at each other, plodding through howling winter wind and driving rain. Briny sea air blows from Cedar Channel. My son is living at Shore Lodge on Cedar Island, just two miles away as the crow flies, in a secure second floor psychiatric unit. When I last visited, Dusty was smoking hot seething angry at seeing me, and he blew a fuse, throwing his walker. Nurse Wright told me not to return until he settles down.

I bite my lip and picture him coming back to this side of the channel, if and when his condition improves. Taking a deep breath of salt air, I steel myself for facing his wrath and his endless firehose of blasting blame. But there's no need to worry now, before trouble rears up from my own flesh and blood. I'll wait and see what's around the bend.

I squeeze Mercury's arm and glance at him, but I barely can see his face, with his baseball cap pulled down low and his rain coat hood up covering his head. Rain lashes at my eyes, and I blink back water droplets.

I say, "Mighty fine day we picked for a walk, isn't it?"

He turns to me and grins. "No one else is out except for us, but I don't mind."

I smile. "We're two old fools, walking the dog on a wild day."

I plod through puddles in my hiking boots and wonder how my niece's road trip is going. Brushing off concerns about her solitary journey, I imagine her stopping for dinner in a diner along the way. I'm sure she's fine. She's probably enjoying herself at this very moment.

3

———————

EMILY

My eyes ache from straining to see in the dark, the defrost fan blows dry air in my face, and I roll up the window. I haven't seen another car in what seems like forever. My eyelids grow heavy, and I'm blinking more than ever. It's time to stop for the night before I cause an accident.

With a frown, I wish I left earlier today, instead of sleeping in, but that's the story of my life. I'd head out the door for work but notice a fascinating spider web in the front hall and stare at it for many minutes before realizing I was late. Or I'd watch television and get sucked into a news story, forgetting about meeting Mellie for a drink, which made her furious. When I start over in a new place, I want to be punctual and a better friend.

A roadside billboard advertises, "Rest a spell at The Gas Station Motel. Try our homemade beef jerky!"

Releasing a sigh, I slow down and round a bend in the road. The Gas Station Motel appears on my right, situated in a vast expanse of vacant land. Bright lights above a gas pump out front of a store make me squint, and beyond that, I see single-story motel rooms.

I brake and pull off the road, parking near the store. Turning off the engine, I lean back against the seat and blow out a breath. My fingers ache from gripping the steering wheel. My hips are stiff from sitting so long in one spot.

I say to my cat, "Here we are, home for the night. I'll get the key to the room and be back before you know it."

Julep meows from her crate on the front seat. My tabby cat is not pleased we're taking this trip, and she'd rather be home in our apartment overlooking the poultry plant. But that's in the past, and we can't go back.

Climbing out of the car, I gently close the door, so as not to disturb my pet. Cool, moist air carries the odor of burning leaves, and dark clouds hover overhead. A change in the weather is coming, as Dad used to say.

A Styrofoam cup rolls on the paved parking lot, pushed by a steady breeze. Stray bits of litter swirl up into the air. Leaves rustle in trees, and I sniff the air, sensing a storm on the way. Prickles of doubt tickle at the back of my mind about staying at this out of the way place.

My eyes are dry from driving so long, and my limbs are heavy. I need a place to crash for the night. I'm exhausted.

I stumble toward the store, and wind ruffles my hair, rushing through trees. A big warehouse is next door to the motel, but that's the only other building around. A neon sign in the window of the motel announces "No Vacancy."

Yanking on the door handle, I step inside a small store. A man with thinning hair in his fifties stands behind the counter. He scratches his stubbled chin with gray whiskers and studies me.

I walk up to the counter and say, "I have a reservation for Workman."

The man tilts his head and looks puzzled, tugging on an earlobe.

I say, "The reservation is for Emily Workman, for tonight."

He scratches his head, and flakes of dandruff drift down to his shoulders. "I thought you were a no-show, so someone else took your room an hour ago."

My mouth falls open. "But I gave my credit card to hold it and said I'd arrive late."

He chomps on a wad of pink gum. "What can I say? A guy came in and offered me more than the going rate." He shrugs. "He was desperate to find a place to stay. I thought you weren't coming, and I couldn't turn down the money."

Shaking my head, I fume at my friend who recommended this out of the way motel. I say, "You must have a spare room you keep for situations like this. I've been driving for hours, and I need to sleep."

A small television on the counter behind him is tuned

to a game show. He looks down and fiddles with a piece of paper. "Sorry, but you wouldn't like what we have available. It's not up to our usual standards, so I can't offer it to you."

I drum my fingers on the counter. "I'll take anything you have. It's just for tonight, and I'll check out early tomorrow, so it won't matter what it looks like."

He clears his throat. "We do have something, but it's not our typical standard room. It's located in an unusual area of the building, and we rarely use it. I don't want to hear any complaints, if you take it."

I cross my arms. "I've got to sleep. I'm beat and need a room. I have my cat with me, as I mentioned when I reserved a pet-friendly room."

"We have a room we don't use often, but the cat can't go in. It's not a pet-friendly room, like the one you reserved. We can't have cat dander contaminating it. Other people have allergies, you know. It's fairly common. My Aunt Edna was allergic to cats. She'd sneeze and use a whole box of tissues if a cat came near her. But she's gone and passed on."

I yawn, and my eyelids are heavy. My body is telling me to go to sleep. I'll sneak my cat in the room, and no one will notice. I don't want her to be out in the cold. I say, "I'm sorry to hear your aunt passed."

He shrugs. "No one liked her much anyways."

I raise my eyebrows. Something about the motel feels off, and I consider calling my aunt Jacklyn for support, but

I brush away the thought. It's late, and I'm an adult. I'll be fine. It's only for one night. I say, "I'll take the room."

He nods. "As long as I don't hear any complaints about it. Give me your credit card."

I hand it over, and he scans it. He pushes two pages across the counter and offers me a pen. "Write down your license plate number, so we won't tow your car during the night. Sign here and initial there."

I initial and sign without reading the fine print, and push the papers back to him. He hands me a key card, and I say, "Where's the room?"

He glances at a wall clock and points down a dimly lit hallway. Florescent overhead lights buzz. "The room is in the back, down the hall. I close at midnight, and that means in five minutes, you must be in your room, or you'll be locked out. The only access is through the store when it's open."

My stomach knots, and I rest a weary hand on it. "I'll be locked in? It doesn't seem safe. What if there's a fire? I couldn't get out."

"Don't worry. You'll be fine. I'll open the store at six in the morning, and you can leave then. You have until ten o'clock sharp to check out."

Rain starts to pour down outside, pelting the store windows, and I tilt my head, mulling over whether to take this odd room at the end of an interior hallway. I could sleep in the car with my cat, or I could drive down the road, despite waves of fatigue washing over me. A sense of something wrong harps at the back of my brain. Get out of here. Drive on. This situation is suspicious.

I drum my fingers on the counter, ignoring a creeping sense of impending danger. I'm beyond tired. I've got to put up my feet and rest. If I continue to drive, it's possible I might fall asleep and run into a telephone pole.

Opening my hands, I say, "If there's a fire, how will I get out?"

"In that event, the doors will open automatically. Feel free to grab a snack on your way out." He chuckles.

Studying him, I frown and glance around. The shelves in the store are bare, except for a thick layer of dust.

He slaps his thigh. "Just kidding. You'd climb out the bathroom window in that event, but we won't have a fire. We're in tip-top condition and adhere to fire codes."

"Climbing out a bathroom window seems wrong. I doubt that's even legal."

He waves a hand. "Don't worry. Nothing will happen. We've been fine, so far. Besides, what did I tell you? No complaints."

I look around the store. A single cookie in a plastic wrapper sits by the cash register, along with a brown banana that has seen better days. Something feels wrong about the room, and is one night's sleep worth risking my life? On the other hand, it is highly unlikely a fire will break out. I'll leave early tomorrow morning, never giving a second thought to this dent in the road. Besides, my friend Mellie recommended the motel.

He leans on the counter. "If you don't want the room, give me back the key. I'll rip up the paperwork and reverse the charges. I don't care. The money goes to some holding company out of state, not in my pocket."

I bite my lower lip and tell myself it's for one night, and no harm will come to me and my cat. I'm being overly cautious and nervous.

He tugs on the bill of his ball cap. "You could drive to the next town, an hour away, and see if you can find a room there at this time of night."

"I don't want to do that, but I'm uneasy about the set up. It doesn't seem safe."

He tips his head back and cackles. "A storm is coming, so you'd best be on your way if you don't want to stop here tonight. Not everyone likes being locked in, so I'll completely understand it if you say no."

I cringe and glance outside. Rain splatters front windows facing the parking lot. My therapy cat is out there, waiting to come inside, get warm and cuddle on my lap.

I glance outside. I don't want to get in the car and look for another motel room many miles away, so it makes sense to stay here tonight. I'll sneak the cat inside when the man's back is turned. It would be cruel if I left Julep in the car, cold and alone, and I need her by my side.

"I'll take the room."

"I hope you'll like it. We don't have many occasions to put that room to use. It's rare we get this busy."

I arch an eyebrow and hope my anxiety won't bubble up during the night. But I've got Julep, so I'll be fine.

As I walk toward the front door, he calls, "Don't take long out there getting your things. I'm about to close. I recorded a baseball game at home and want to watch it."

Hurrying out to the car, driving rain drips in my eyes, and I can barely see through the downpour. I yank open the car door, grab my suitcase and wrap my coat around the cat crate. "Come on, sweet girl. I'll need your help to get through the night."

Rain fogs my glasses. Making my way to the store, I hope the bed pillows won't be overstuffed ones that will put a crick my neck. A gust of wind lifts my hair, blasting cold rain on my bare neck. A shiver runs up my spine, and I shudder, sensing I have much bigger problems ahead of me than the size and shape of a pillow.

4

———————

EMILY

Lugging the cat carrier and suitcase, I yank open the store door and hurry past the man at the counter, striding down a dim hall. I insert a metal key in the door, the lock clicks open, and I make my way inside. My pulse quickens, and I close the door, not wanting the man at the counter to see my cat. I flick the deadbolt shut and flip on an overhead light, looking around a small room.

A double bed, a side table with a ceramic lamp and a television mounted on the wall offer a simple, spartan, spare room feeling to the furniture My cat meows, and I murmur, "Hush, we'll be fine. It'll be all right."

But my lower lip quivers at this odd set up, where I'll be locked in until morning. I say in a tight voice, "This'll work for tonight. We'll be on our way early tomorrow, no matter what."

I set the cat carrier on the bed and check the bathroom. Ripping back a shower curtain, I let out a whoosh of breath when I see no one is hiding there. I fling open the bathroom window and inspect the opening. All I see is a dark warehouse next door. If I must, I'll stand on the toilet seat, put Mint Julep out the window and then I'll climb out.

I shrug and tell myself the motel will be fine. I'm worried for no reason. Nothing creepy will happen, and Mellie was right to recommend the motel. It's located on the route she suggested, and I was lucky to nab their last little-used room.

My mouth is dry, and I go in the bathroom. Turning on the tap, I fill a plastic cup with water and take a healthy swig. But the water tastes like sulfur, and I cough, bending over the sink and spitting it out.

Wrinkling my nose, I wipe my mouth on a white fluffy towel. I'm in the middle of nowhere, so maybe this is well water, and they need a better filter.

A plastic water bottle sits by the sink on a white paper coaster. A small printed sign states: This water bottle is a free gift. Thank you for staying with us.

I open the bottle, sniff the water, which smells faintly of strawberries, and gulp it down. Turning off the overhead light, I shuffle to bed. Every bone in my body tells me it's time to sleep, but I give my cat nibbles of food and sips of water, leaving on the end table light.

Collapsing on a firm mattress, I rest my head on a hard

pillow and yawn, pulling up the covers. A wave of fatigue washes over me, and I whisper, "I'll close my eyes for a bit, then I'll turn off the light. Everything will be better in the morning."

5

JACKLYN

The evening, Mercury and I go out for dinner, leaving Buddy behind with a dog biscuit. A gregarious family owns the local Italian restaurant, and a smiling gray-haired father welcomes us with open arms, taking us to a table. Sliding into a seat, I glance at the yellow walls giving cheer, where a bar with black walls and a dance floor once occupied the space.

A candle on the table flickers when someone opens the front door, bringing in cool moist air from outside, and I shiver. A few feet from our table, the father says in a booming voice, "Irena, my love, welcome. I'll get your order."

I lean over and say to Mercury, who is studying the menu in candlelight, "If our Irena is here to pick up food, let's invite her to sit with us. She's been all alone since Kelly left for Grand Island."

He nods. "Okay, but you'd better move fast, before she leaves."

I leap to my feet and stride to the front, and sure enough, Irena is waiting for an order to go. She taps a foot, ever in a hurry, and looks at her phone.

I tap her shoulder, and she jerks. She clutches her phone, which she almost dropped, and claps a hand to her chest. "You gave me a fright. I didn't expect to see you here. It's such a dark, rainy night, I thought no one else would be out."

I gesture to our table. "Mercury and I just arrived. Come join us. We'd love to share a meal with you and hear about what you and Kelly are up to."

Pursing her lips, she scuffs a foot. "I'll let you two have a romantic dinner by yourselves. I don't want to impose."

"Nonsense, come join us. I insist. I've been meaning to call you, because I have something to ask you."

She nods, but a flicker of distaste flicks across her face before she wipes it away. I hope I haven't become a pest with my friends, but I'm sure she'll want to hear more about the tiny home project and the dog park, because she's taking care of a dog while two friends recover from a car crash and a traumatic brain injury.

We tell the host at the front desk about our plans to dine together, and soon, the three of us are settled around a candlelit table, drinking wine. I put down my glass and fiddle with my hands in my lap. This isn't the best time to broach the topic of money and ask Irena to invest in my tiny home project, but there will never be a perfect time. I'll dive in and get the job done before our food arrives.

6

———

IRENA

I hop out of my car, slam the door shut and hurry through the wind and rain into an Italian restaurant. Closing the door behind me, I inhale mouth-watering aromas coming from the kitchen. I detect garlic sizzling, tomato sauce cooking, and perhaps meatballs simmering in a pan. Warm air welcomes me, and an older man with gray hair greets me by name. My home is empty without my daughter, who moved to Grand Island to attend school and escape bullies in town. In this cozy restaurant, I'm surrounded by jovial people in a bustling place, where I don't feel as alone.

A gray-haired host smiles, opening his arms. "Irena, good to see you. I'll get your order."

While I wait, I pull out my phone and check to see if Kelly texted me back. Seeing no new messages, I sigh. My close-knit group of high school friends broke up like a boat on the rocks when Buzz jumped off Jackson Bridge, and Craig went to prison. I feel like I'm the only one left, carrying out routine tasks of running a rescue boat business, except now my beautiful teenage daughter isn't by my side when I'm at the helm.

Someone taps me on the shoulder from behind, and I flinch. My phone falls from my hands, but I grab the device before it hits the floor. Shoving it in my pocket, I turn and see my friend Jacklyn. Her cheeks are rosy, and she's smiling. Her sparkling scoop neck blouse tells me she dressed up for the occasion, but her mismatched socks and hiking boots look more fitting for a trek in the mountains than dinner in a restaurant. But then again, our town is casual, so you can come as you are and get away with it, which is just my style.

Jacklyn says in a kind voice, "I'm sorry, I didn't mean to startle you. Mercury and I are at a table right over there. Come join us, and we'll catch up. I'd like to hear how you and Kelly are doing."

I swallow hard, hearing my daughter's name, reminded of her empty bedroom at home. I never noticed the hollow sound my footsteps make in the hall before she left to stay with our friend Tex. Making dinner for one isn't as much fun when your special person is a boat ride away. Shaking my head, I say, "I wouldn't want to interrupt your romantic dinner together."

Jacklyn points to a table, where Mercury waves. A red bow tie is clipped to his long gray beard, and he's wearing a dark vest over a white shirt with rolled up sleeves. I tilt my head and mull over her offer. "I was heading home to eat there."

She pats my shoulder. "Please join us. I've been remiss in not calling you, and I want to hear how you're doing. But I also want to ask you something."

I cringe at the idea of her asking me something, but I nod. With a shrug, I agree to eat with them, and we arrange for my lasagna to be served at the table. Following Jacklyn to where Mercury is seated, I stop myself from rolling my eyes. I bet she wants to pester me a second time for Tex's contact information to drum up investors for her building project. When Jacklyn gets ahold of an idea, she doesn't let go, just like her son. She'd never admit to the similarity, but it's glaringly clear to me. Dusty and Jacklyn both have lantern jaws, fire in their eyes when they're riled up, and they're stubborn beyond belief.

I take a seat beside Jacklyn and across from Mercury. I'm glad she admitted Dusty to Shore Lodge, because I have the feeling if he was released, he'd rain hellfire down on his mother. She tried her best, and if there were parenting failures, they weren't all her fault. Much of the responsibility, from what I hear, rests with Jacklyn's deceased husband, Albert, who trained their son Dusty to depend on handouts to survive and fill his construction company coffers, which is not the way to run a business. I'm no expert, but even I know that.

Mercury pats the table, and his exposed forearms with

shirt sleeves rolled up look strong. "Glad you decided to join us. What are you having?"

I smile. "Thanks for inviting me. I'm having lasagna, and it'll be enough for two dinners."

Jacklyn leans over and nudges my arm. "Want to share a salad?"

I arch an eyebrow, because I haven't been eating well since Kelly left. I've been in more of a take-out and Thai food with a beer kind of mood. Thank goodness they mostly retired a talking robot at one restaurant, because that gave me a headache. "Sure, sharing a salad is a good idea."

She smiles. "Are you okay with a Caesar salad? You'll breathe garlic like a dragon for days."

I shrug. "There's no one else but me in the house or boat these days, so I can breathe garlic breath, and no one will notice."

A cheerful waiter with round cheeks and a mop of brown hair brings over a white board listing specials, and he reels off a long list of items. Although they sound delicious, I'm pleased I picked the tried-and-trusted hearty lasagna. Jacklyn and Mercury place their orders, and the round-cheeked waiter leaves. When Jacklyn turns to me, I suspect she's about to pounce on the topic of money, but she says, "I've been thinking about you. I bet your house feels lonely without Kelly living there."

I nod. "It's been more difficult than I expected, but I'm getting through it. Ice cream at night is my medicine. I wish Abby was back at work, bringing home cartons from the ice cream factory, but she's still home recovering from the car accident."

Jacklyn raises her eyebrows. "Abby and Jack are going through a tough time, but at least they have each other. And I know all about comfort food during difficult times. Nothing's the same when someone you love is gone."

Mercury clears his throat. "We should get together for dinner once a week, until Kelly returns. Is she coming home for the summer?"

I wince. "She wants to stay on Grand Island for the summer, but I'm not a fan of the idea. I want her back in town, and so do Abby and Jack. Right now, they can barely do anything, given Abby's car wreck, and Jack's head injury."

The waiter brings our salads, and we squeeze lemon wedges over romaine lettuce and dig in. The tart flavor of lemon juice makes my mouth pucker. Fresh shaved parmesan cheese melts in my mouth, and I taste a hint of anchovy in the creamy dressing.

Mercury says, "I've known Jack for years. We used to meet at the marina and talk on a bench for hours."

I drum my fingers on the table. "So, that's where where he was, when he wasn't home helping me with Kelly. Did he tell you how he left to attend sneaker conventions without letting me know?"

Mercury sits back and stares at his wine glass, twirling it, and I tell myself to tone down my ire. If I don't, this dinner will become difficult to digest. I say, "I'm sorry, I shouldn't take it out on you for what Jack did when we were married. The blame rests solely on his shoulders."

Mercury nods and leans forward, sipping wine. "He didn't want me to meet you or speak with you about what he told me in confidence. If he'd given me the all-clear signal, I'd have reached out to you, and we could have shared our concerns. By the way, how is his sneaker addiction? Has he gotten control of it?"

"Abby says he hasn't mentioned sneakers since he left the hospital. He doesn't remember how to get online or use a smart phone, so we're safe for now from his old habits of hoarding high-end sneakers. I want him to recover and get a job, because I'd like the ten years' back child support he owes me."

Jacklyn and Mercury frown, and I say, "I'm about at the end of my rope waiting for it. Raising a child isn't cheap. But you can't make a dead man cough up money, and he was definitely near death. I only have so much patience, and if he doesn't rally by late spring and find work, I'll meet with an attorney to see what recourse I have."

Mercury says, "What's he thinking of doing for work? I'd ask him myself, but he doesn't remember who I am, given his amnesia."

I set down my fork on my empty salad plate and shrug. "He wants to work in a hospital and help sick people, maybe as an ultrasound or X-ray tech. The other day he mentioned getting trained to draw blood, so he's not sure."

Jacklyn pats my shoulder. "He'll find something. Abby will push him in the right direction."

I take a deep breath. "She will. She understands how important this is. I could do more to help Kelly, like pay for additional counselling sessions, if I had that money."

A server takes our salad plates and leaves. Jacklyn says, "What about the money Buzz had in his investment accounts? I assumed you inherited that, along with his house, his boat, and the bookstore."

My pulse picks up, and I press my lips together, not wanting to give away a scintilla of my secret that Buzz survived his fall from Jackson Bridge. No one must know that he recently showed up in town and left, after saying goodbye to me. By now, he should be in another town starting over. I gnaw on my lower lip and hope I did the right thing by not telling people he's alive.

I clear my throat. "I didn't get any of his money, and I don't even know how much there was. It went to a charity that helps kids who are bullied in school, like we were."

The waiter serves our dinners, and steam rises from my lasagna, giving off aromas of garlic, tomato sauce, pasta and cheese. Delicious smells wafting from our plates on the table do little to quell my fears that these two brilliant minds will somehow ferret out the fact that Buzz is alive.

To distract them, I say, "In grade school, Buzz and I

were taunted for our names, and that's how we became friends. Before I married Jack and became Irena Fishbone, my name was Irena Pickle."

Jacklyn puts down her fork. "That must've been difficult. Kids pick on people with funny names."

I cut into my lasagna. "Yep, that was our fate in fourth grade. It was fated that Irena Pickle and Bud Weiser were forever to be friends."

Mercury smiles. "I'm one up on you, almost, with my name. Mercury Thunder put a target on my back all through my life."

Jacklyn waves her fork in the air. "I was teased for my last name, Stone, but I'm sure it was nothing like what you two went through." A look of concern crosses her face. "My son says he'll never forgive me for naming him Dusty Stone. Kids taunted him in the playground and wouldn't let it go. So, I'm glad Buzz gave his money to a cause like that, helping kids being bullied. It's an insidious problem that's difficult to stomp out."

"It is." Pushing thoughts of my daughter being bullied by school mates in town from my mind, I take a bite of delectable lasagna. The delicious, complex flavors make me moan.

Jacklyn says, "The food's good, isn't it? I'm sorry to hear you didn't inherit money from Buzz, because I was going to ask you if you'd like to invest in my new tiny home project."

Mercury arches an eyebrow, perhaps feeling as I do,

that this is not a discussion to have over a pleasant dinner, when we're catching up. But this is an important part of her life, so I'll listen to what she has to say about it. If I don't, she'll just corner me another time. I might as well get it over with.

With a little sigh, I set down my fork, wipe my mouth on a cloth napkin and say, "Tell me about it. I'm all ears."

7

JACKLYN

Mercury taps a spatulated finger on his wine glass, perhaps to get my attention and stop me from charging ahead and telling Irena about my tiny home project. But I have a head of steam going, and I blunder ahead, ignoring warning signs from Irena, who lets out a little sigh and wipes her mouth on a napkin. I want to get this over with before the meal ends, so we can continue sharing stories about our lives.

I wave my hands in the air and bump Irena's arm as she reaches for her wine glass. She puts her palms on the table top, as if bracing for impact, and I bumble ahead. "I'm looking for one or two investors who would be silent partners for my tiny homes and dog park project on a hill overlooking town. The plot of land has water views looking west to the San Juan Islands and north to Cedar Channel, toward Canada. It'll be a gorgeous place to live.

The homes will be compact but comfortable spaces for one or two people to live, complete with plumbing and running water."

Irena crosses her arms. "Well, I hope so. Running water and plumbing are pretty important, when you're buying a home."

I grin. "Yes, you're right. And the views looking west to the San Juans are stunning. You might want to sell your home and move into one of them."

She rolls her eyes. "I like my home just fine, thanks. And I'm sorry to tell you, but all my money is tied up in my boat business. Whatever savings I have, I'm keeping in reserve for Kelly, in case she decides to go to college, although that's a long ways off."

Her phone buzzes, and she glances at a text. Turning to us, Irena says, "Sorry, but I have to go help a boater in distress. You're welcome to take the rest of my dinner with you to eat later. I've got to run."

She stands and waves a credit card at our waiter, but I jump up and say, "I'll pay for your meal. It's the least I can do after ambushing you and making you listen to my sales pitch."

She brushes hair from her eyes. "I'll tell other people about it, but right now, I'm out of here. Thanks for dinner. I'll see you later."

She strides out of the restaurant, hustling Irena-style in a hurried manner, and I sink into a seat across from Mercury. "Well, I blew that, didn't I?"

He cocks his head. "Who knew a boater would call for help just then?"

I open my hands. "She's always on call. It must be a stressful way to live."

He shrugs. "But she seems happy with it. That's all that matters."

I nod. "At least I got my message across, loud and clear."

He grins. "It was loud and clear, all right. I think the couple at the next table heard about it, you were so enthusiastic."

A woman in her thirties with long brown hair gets up from a nearby table. She comes over to us and says, "Did I hear you talking about building tiny homes in Millersville? With views?"

My eyebrows shoot up. "Yes, and I'm starting a wait list for people who are interested and willing to put down a deposit. I'll build the homes, and people can pick out counter tops and faucets. You'll have to buy your own appliances, of course."

She shifts from side to side. "I'm a school teacher, and I'd love to live near town in a tiny home. Can you put me on your list? How far down will I be? I really want this."

I stand and reach out to pat her hand. "You'll be fifth on the list."

She beams. "Great, my name is Myra Bird. Here's my contact information."

I add it to notes on my phone, and we chat for a bit

before I say, "Wonderful to meet you, Myra, and I'll be in touch about the deposit and details. I'm glad you're as excited as I am about this project."

A wide smile spreads across her face. "This is going to be perfect for me. It's what I've been looking for. I didn't want to buy land and hire someone to build it. This is a relief. I'm glad we bumped into each other tonight."

I shake her hand. "Tell everyone you can think of who might be interested. If you have a dog, they'll love the fenced dog park we're putting in."

Her eyes open wide. "I've wanted to get a dog, but haven't yet. I love it."

We part ways, and I pay the bill. Mercury and I walk to the car, buffeted by wind and lashed by cold rain. He says, "Better get the permits before you make promises you can't keep. Don't oversell, or you might come to regret it."

I climb into the driver's seat and start the car. "Good point, and I was thinking the same thing. Tomorrow morning, I'll contact an engineer to see how many units I can fit on the land. But I don't want it to feel cramped and crowded."

"But this is a business proposition, not a consensus circle, where everyone feels good about the outcome. You need to turn a profit, as you know from owning your garden store. If you don't, you might go bust and lose your bungalow."

I frown and turn a corner, heading for my home. In my wildest dreams, I'd hoped the building plan would make everyone happy, with no conflict, and money would fall from the sky. I snort, as if that would ever happen. Some people like to argue, no matter what the circumstances. I'll attempt to weed out contentious knuckle heads at the outset. My son fits that description, and he'd stir up a ruckus, even if I went to the moon and back to please him. If I'm honest with myself, I'm glad he's at Shore Lodge, on the other side of the channel, and out of my hair.

Parking in my driveway, I say, "I guess the plan doesn't have to be perfect, but one that works for my pocketbook and buyers. Would you like to take Buddy on a walk with me and come in for a night cap?"

He gives me a smile and cracks open the car door. "I thought you'd never ask. One of my favorite things to do is to walk Buddy in the wind and rain, because I feel alive with each step, by your side."

"Aren't I the lucky one?"

"No, I'm the lucky one."

I grin. "Let's argue about that later and take Buddy for his last walk. I hope Irena is doing okay on the water tonight. The wind sure is blowing."

8

IRENA

Plowing through rough seas in the dark, I aim my spotlight on the water and search for a floundering sailboat near Washington Park. Rain drums down on my boat deck, and wind whips past, buffeting the boat. Burrows Island appears out of the gloom, and my spotlight catches on a twenty-five-foot sailboat wallowing in two-foot chop. Frothy white capped waves crash up against the sides of the boat. The boat bobs up and down, and tosses back and forth, and I shake my head. Welcome to the carnival ride of boating in blustery weather.

Holding a marine radio microphone, I hail the boat in distress. "Seabreeze, Seabreeze, Seabreeze, come in please. This is the rescue boat Nimbus calling. I'm off your bow."

"Nimbus, this is Seabreeze. We need a tow to the marina. It's too rough for us."

"Understood. I'll come alongside soon. Over and out."

I turn my wheel and steer my boat next to the sailboat, dropping fenders and tying my lines off at his midship. The skipper, a man in his forties with a receding hairline and flushed cheeks, waves a hand. "We came out for a sunset cruise with drinks, but the weather got the better of us. My motor doesn't have the oomph to get us back to shore."

I nod, and the boats bob up and down in the sea. "After I take your payment, I'll give you a tow. Are you wanting to go to the Millersville Marina or Skyline, right over there?"

He blows out a breath and pulls out his wallet, handing over a credit card. "I've got a slip in Skyline, so let's go there. It's not far, but I couldn't make it on my own."

I tap his card to my phone and hand it back. "That's settled. Put on your personal floatation devices, and I'll get going."

He names an area of the marina that's difficult to reach, with a narrow fairway, and I nod. "I'll get you in there. Just sit back and enjoy the ride."

Forty minutes later, the under-powered sailboat is tucked in a slip, and I putter away in my boat, exiting the marina and heading past Burrows Island. With a sigh, I turn the wheel and head toward the marina in Millersville.

Docking my boat in my home slip a few blocks from downtown, I hop in my car, not bothering to wash down the boat for once. At my house, I run a hot bath. I'm about to climb in and looking forward to soaking the day away, when my phone dings.

Kelly texts, 'Are you awake?'

My fingers fly as I respond. 'Sure am. I miss you, sweet girl.'

'Miss you too, Mom.'

'Want to talk now?'

"No, I'm supposed to be asleep. Tomorrow though.'

I smile and wipe tears from my cheeks. 'Tomorrow it is. Sleep well, love.'

'You too.'

Shucking off my clothes, I step into the tub and let warm water soothe the aches and pains in my body and heart. Tomorrow will be better. And the one after that will be even better. I can bet on that.

9

EMILY

Cold fingers press on the back of my hand, and a woman says in a stern voice, "Wake up." I open my eyes and squint at a bright overhead light, feeling confused and wondering if I'm at my aunt's house and overslept. I move my hands to rub my eyes but discover my right wrist is shackled to the railing of a hospital bed.

My gut churns, and my mouth drops open. I'm dressed in a hospital gown. The double bed, side table, and television on the wall are missing, as is my cat in her carrier. Everything is wrong.

My pulse races. A red curtain is pulled around the bed, and I squirm, looking for my cat. Plastic under me crinkles. I must be dreaming, so I pinch my thumb and index finger together and drive a fingernail into bare skin, wincing in pain. This, unfortunately, is real, and I'm awake in a different room.

I grimace, picturing someone moving my body, changing my clothes and taking my precious pet. Did my friend Mellie set me up for an elaborate practical joke? If so, it's not funny. I was drugged, and someone moved me while I slept.

My body shudders, and I scream, yanking at the wrist restraint. My gaze flits around a sterile cold room, and a horrible thought snakes into my brain. They might be about to operate on me.

A middle-aged woman with a helmet of stiff shoulder-length brown hair stands at the bedside, watching me and frowning. A chill creeps up my spine, and my hands turn clammy. I say in a hoarse voice, "Who are you and why are you doing this? Let me go."

She crosses her arms. "You're about to participate in an experiment, and then you'll donate a kidney. My associates will join us soon."

"A kidney? You can't do that. It's against the law." I attempt to leap out of bed, but the plastic wrist restraint stops me, yanking me back, digging into my flesh, cutting my skin.

I swallow hard, and my mind races. I've read about criminals targeting vulnerable people out of work, like I am, and cutting out kidneys and livers to sell them on the black market. Gritting my teeth, I make a vow. I won't let them touch me or my cat. "I won't let you operate on me."

She taps a toe. "Yes, you will. We know you're unemployed and need money, and we'll pay you very well for your kidney."

Goosebumps prick my flesh, imagining someone cutting into my belly and conducting major surgery on me. "I'll find a job soon. I don't need your stinking money."

"We'll make it worth it to you. You'll help someone who needs a kidney but is way down on a regular organ wait list. People are desperate, and they'll pay top dollar. You'll be glad you did this, because we'll pay you for donating an organ voluntarily. But you must sign the consent forms first."

I clench my teeth. "No, I'll make my money another way. Let me go."

"The operation won't hurt and you'll recover right away, with no negative side effects. The kidney will grow back. and we'll give you money."

Squirming in the bed, trying to free my wrist, I shake my head. "Donating a kidney is a huge operation, and kidneys don't grow back. Stop lying and release me and give me back my cat."

She checks her phone and nods. "Consent is critical for organ donation, and we take our responsibilities seriously. You'll sign two consent forms. One is for a clinical trial, where you're going to be the last subject enrolled in the study. You'll also sign a second form to donate your kidney."

I swallow hard. My hands tremble. My armpits prick with sweat, despite the cool temperature of the room. "I'm not doing this, and I won't sign. Where is my cat? I need her, right now."

Helmet Hair pulls on a pair of blue disposable gloves. "Your cat is being kept in a safe place. You can see her after you sign the forms."

Sweat trickles down my arms. I tip my head back and yell. "I want to see my cat."

A tall man with dark hair wearing a white lab coat pushes open a red curtain. He's about my age, in his mid-twenties, and carrying a clipboard. Behind him, I catch a glimpse of two other patients in hospital beds, an older woman and a gray-haired, grizzled man, both wearing hospital gowns and looking dazed.

The tall man closes the curtain and turns to me. On his white lab coat, blue embroidered letters show a name, Nathan Fletcher. He stands at the foot of the bed. "Hello. I trust you slept well?"

He taps a pen against a clipboard, and I wrinkle my forehead, where a headache throbs. I hope my aunt will realize I'm missing and come find me, although it would be an impossible task for her to track me down. Only Mellie knows where I am.

I bite my lip, and it dawns on me that I can't sit and wait for my aunt to show up. By the time help arrives, it'll be too late, and my cat and I will be dead.

Criminals are about to cut into my body to remove an organ, and I must find a way out.

10

NATHAN FLETCHER

Looking into a young woman's brown eyes, a feeling of dread sweeps over me. This final subject in our study is named Emily Workman, and she is unemployed, like many of the people we target for organ donation. My father's voice reaches up from the grave, telling me to run before I allow her to join the others who have died on the operating table. She looks like a nice person. I shouldn't be part of this scheme or coerce her to join my scientific study.

My throat is dry, and I swallow. When I was first offered this research position to augment my teaching wages, I jumped at the chance and signed up right away, without conducting due diligence and thoroughly checking who I'd be working with. The simple truth is, I blundered into a crime ring preying on vulnerable individuals like Emily to take their kidneys and livers.

Chewing on the inside of my cheek, I deeply regret joining this group of criminals. But after all I've seen and done, they won't let me leave. I've seen people left on the operating table post-surgery, where they're expected to recover on their own, without medical assistance. I'm as guilty as they are, although I don't wield a scalpel, and I bear the heavy burden and responsibility for many deaths, all in the name of making more money.

I tap my pen on a clipboard and blame myself. If this falls apart, it's my fault, because I naively joined them. They brought me into their organ harvesting scheme, paying me money for my silence, and I suggested we layer on a scientific study to test an anxiety medication for possible use on organ donors to calm their nerves before operations. My experiment involves giving one control arm group a placebo, or sugar pill, while the other half will receive the test drug.

Releasing a slow breath, I wish I was anywhere but here and without ambition and debts left by my dad before his demise. My dreams are haunted, because when patients wake up after operations, we ignore their screaming howls of pain and flee the premises, leaving them to die or survive on their own.

11

———

EMILY

Yanking on a plastic wrist restraint, but not breaking it in two, I say to the man in the white lab coat, "Where am I? And where's my cat? Who are you and why are you doing this?"

"We're conducting a clinical trial," he says. "There's nothing to worry about."

I blink and try to clear the fog from my brain. I want to find a way to jump out of bed and leave this room behind. I don't have my glasses, and Aunt Jacklyn isn't here to help. Neither is Mellie, who I'm beginning to suspect was in on all of this from the beginning. I don't know how, but I must extract myself from this situation, find my cat and run for my car.

I cough and say, "I was drugged and moved. This is illegal, and I'll report you. Give me back my cat and my glasses."

I swing my legs over the side of the bed, but my movements are slow, and my mind is muzzy from whatever they put in the water bottle and maybe later by injection when I was knocked out in bed.

The woman with a helmet of brown hair appears to be in charge. She marches over, pushes me back in bed and restrains my other wrist to the bed rail. I scream, squirm and writhe, but they stand and stare at me. From the way they're looking at me, I'm just another specimen, and I doubt appealing to their higher instincts will open any doors. I've got to come up with a plan.

Glancing around the sterile hospital-like setting, I'm reminded of how I got into this mess in the first place. My supposed friend Mellie suggested I stay here. What, I wonder, did she have to gain by steering me to this motel? I don't know the answer or what they're up to, but they have the upper hand, and I'm tied down, with both wrists lashed to a hospital bed.

Breathing hard, I'm light-headed. If my therapy cat was here, she'd calm me down, but I don't know where she is. Fletcher and Helmet Hair watch me. They're quiet, as if waiting for someone to arrive.

A man parts the curtains and comes to my bedside, and my mouth drops open. This guy worked at the front counter at the motel when I checked in.

Patting his thinning hair, he says, "This patient is a good one. We need younger donors. Not many buyers want organs from older folks."

Fletcher nods. "Baby boomers drive through, taking bucket list trips, heading to see the ocean. Too many of them, if you ask me."

Helmet Hair steps close. "We'll draw your blood for tests, but don't worry. It won't hurt."

Every nerve in my body ignites, triggering a fight or flight reaction. I kick her, and Helmet Hair steps back, glaring. She says to the other two, "I told you we should've put in an IV when she was asleep."

Counter Guy turns to Fletcher. "She needs to sign the consent forms."

I frown. "I'm not signing anything, so you can forget it."

Fletcher wipes his brow with a trembling hand, saying to the others, "I know we have to do this, but it doesn't seem right."

Helmet Hair scowls. "Get her to sign the forms, now."

He walks up to me and says, "I'm sorry. I didn't realize exactly what they doing when I took this job. But you can have your cat back if you sign these papers."

"Give me my cat and my glasses, and let me go."

Fletcher shoves the clipboard and pen at me and says in a low voice, "It'll be easier on you if you sign right here and there. I'll get your cat after you sign, and we'll release you."

Counter Guy smirks, covering his mouth with his hand.

Helmet Hair waves a hand in front of her face. "Just sign the forms. If you don't, worse things will happen."

I tug at my wrists, tied to bed railings, but the restraints don't budge. I wish I'd never left my hometown, even though nothing was left for me there. I would have stayed longer, if not forever, in Mellie's spare bedroom, but she told me it was time to move on and I'd overstayed my welcome. I cried myself to sleep that night and called aunt Jacklyn the next morning.

I said in a hoarse voice, "Hi Aunt Jacklyn, this is your niece Emily."

"Hello, Emily."

Before she could say anything else, I blurted out, "I know it's been a long time since I saw you, but can I come stay with you while I look for a job in Millersville? I know it's a lot to ask, but I have to find a new place to stay. And I have a cat. I have nowhere else to go."

My aunt said, "Of course you can stay with me. How soon can you come?"

"If it's okay, I'll leave tomorrow and be there the day after."

"That soon? Well, fine, come join the party. We'll have a good time. I have a dog, but he's pretty special, and he likes cats, so don't worry about Buddy."

We said goodbye, and I hung up, fresh tears trickling down my cheeks. One person in the world loved me and welcomed me. One was enough. That's all I needed, besides my cat.

Now, Helmet Hair presses her lips together, and her hands clench. Pointing to the red curtain, she says, "Do you want to end up like those two? They didn't sign the consent forms and look what happened to them. Rip back the red curtain, Fletcher, and show her."

He opens the curtain, and my jaw drops. Two older people are drooling, chins on their chests, with their eyes closed. Their shackled hands hang limp. If these two older people are trapped beyond belief, there's no hope for me.

12

COUNTER GUY

The young woman procrastinates, and I'm growing impatient. I'm on a deadline and have to get back to staff the motel front desk soon. We've got another group of travelers coming through tonight, and we picked a fresh victim to schedule for our special services. When she called and made her reservation, I was able to look up her age and bad habits healthwise. The power of the name, address and phone number go a long ways in helping us to find the right people to target. After Emily, the foot dragger with excuses, our next donor will be a woman in her forties traveling alone and a nonsmoker, which our client on the black market requires.

Emily pleads to be released. She's young and innocent, but today's events in the operating suite will change that.

If she survives the operation, she'll be lucky if she can drive away.

She's a trouble maker, though, I sense it. We might have to take her out to the back field to bury her remains with her beloved cat that tried to bite me when I picked up the cat carrier earlier. Good riddance to both of them. The cat can be kitty in a blender for all I care, and their bodies will blend in with the soil as fertilizer, the sooner the better.

13

HELMET HAIR

The two idiots who were assigned to work with me don't know what they're doing. I'd like to chuck them out to the parking lot and send them packing, but I need their help to get this girl's consent, before I assist the physician for the operation. I check my phone and see the doctor is thirty minutes late. It's difficult to find dependable help these days. If I had ready replacements, I'd fire the doctor and these two losers.

I clench my teeth and count to ten to calm myself. We'll finish with Emily, who seems to specialize in blinking her eyes, and let her go with money in her pocket and threats to keep quiet. I'll talk with my boss, so she'll understand we need professionals, not people who run home to watch a ballgame on television instead of helping me last night. And Nathan is nervous, which riles up the patient. We must sound sure of ourselves to get her consent.

I nod to myself. A physician on the other end of the transaction will insist on seeing her consent form before accepting her kidney and paying us. This is tough work, and not everyone is cut out for it, but I like the money.

Glancing at the time, I realize we're running behind schedule. We've got to pick up the pace, with no more acting nice. We'll make her sign the consent forms.

14

EMILY

Fletcher glances at two older gray-haired people in beds, and a flicker of concern crosses his face. He turns and stares at me with deep brown eyes, biting his lower lip.

I try to rip off the restraints, but to no avail. My wrists throb, and plastic bands cut into my skin. I say, "You should be ashamed of yourselves, tricking me and taking an innocent animal away from her owner. Why are you doing this?"

Fletcher shrugs. "I need the money. My mom's sick, and my dad died."

I run my tongue across my dry lips. He sounds vulnerable, so he might understand my plight and help release me. If I can get the other two to leave, I'll speak with Fletcher and convince him to give me my cat and let us slip out the door.

Helmet Hair says, "Remember, Fletcher, you need to publish to get tenure at the university. They're breathing down your neck and keeping track of how many research papers you publish in peer-reviewed journals. Let's get going and finish what we started. She's the last subject in our experiment."

A chill sweeps over me, and goosebumps prick my arms. I shriek, but the walls soak up the sound. I glance around for my phone to call for help but frown, because of course, the criminals took my phone.

I say, "This is unethical, and I'll report you to the authorities."

Counter Guy chuckles. "We have authorities in our pockets, and they won't believe you or care. How do you think we've gotten away with this for so long?"

Helmet Hair smiles. "We looked into your background. You have no family, only one friend and an animal to keep you company. You're alone with no one to rescue you, so you're a perfect target. No one will care if you're gone. So, calm down. If you cooperate, you'll get your cat back. Just let us conduct the experiment."

My pulse quickens, because I hate being told to calm down. If my hands were free, I'd knock her flat on the floor and run from this terrible place. "I won't sign away my rights."

She says, "Fletcher, get her to sign the forms, so we can get this last patient treated and processed. The deadline for submitting the paper is tomorrow morning."

Fletcher nods and taps a pen on his clipboard. "Sign here and there. That's all you have to do. Sign the two forms, and then you can have your cat."

Watching them, I sense I have a temporary advantage. If I sign, I'll surrender the little power I have. Aiming for the ultimate goalpost, I say, "Cut off these restraints and set me free with my cat. You can finish your study without me. After I leave, I won't tell a soul what you're doing here."

Counter Guy stands with his hands in front, fig-leaf style. "We're not letting you go, so just give up that idea. Besides, if you don't sign, your cat will die, and it'll be your fault."

My body breaks out in a cold sweat. "Please, don't do that. Be kind to her. She doesn't deserve that."

Counter Guy says, "Then sign the papers and do it now. Or we'll hurt your cat."

Fletcher says in a trembling voice, "This isn't right. Threats aren't how we obtain consent. I don't want to coerce any more subjects in our study because we're on a tight deadline. It's not the right way to do things."

I press my lips together and don't say a word. Fletcher is siding with me, which is promising. My breathing slows, knowing I might have an ally.

Counter Guy shrugs. "She needs a push to get going." Turning to me, he says, "Sign now, or you and your cat will disappear down the long drive out back, buried in a field like the others, where they'll never find you."

Tears trickle down my cheeks. I vowed to keep my cat safe when I adopted her three years ago. I don't matter, and no one will miss me, probably not even Aunt Jacklyn. She might be relieved not to have a freeloader like me in her home, endlessly looking for jobs that don't materialize, like Mellie was when she kicked me out. But I can't let anything happen to Mint Julep, my tabby cat. She's an innocent animal and didn't do anything wrong.

Helmet Hair says, "Your precious cat will die if you don't sign the consent forms. Your cat is depending on you. Save a feline's life and sign on the dotted line."

I cock my head, mulling over what to do. If I could free my hands, I'd escape, but that isn't possible, not yet. A thought flits past, and I frown, wondering if my friend Mellie had any idea what was going on at the motel when she sent me here. She's the sole reason I picked the place. But no, she wouldn't do that. She's too good a friend to betray me. She'd protect me with her last breath.

A headache throbs, and I recall how Mellie booted me out of her house and almost glared at me before I left. There should be warnings and complaints plastered online about these maniacs conducting experiments and operating on motel guests, but I didn't see any. I'm in a secret, soundproof place far away from others, and no one will find me in time. I'm not sure if Mellie was part of this scheme, but it doesn't do me any good to focus on her moral culpability. The people in front of me are in control, and I must find a crack in their plans, slither through a crevice and escape, bringing them down.

Fletcher says to me in a soft voice, "What happens next is up to you. You get to pick if your cat lives or dies."

My heart races. I gulp and listen for the sound of my cat meowing, but all is quiet, except for the ringing in my ears. My body trembles at the horror of my untenable choice. If I sacrifice myself, I'll save my cat, and I must do that.

Pointing to the consent papers, Counter Guy says, "Stop messing around and wasting time. Sign the damn forms and get it over with."

15

JACKLYN

First thing in the morning, I call the engineer who drew up plans for Stone Estates, and when he answers, I say, "Hello, this is Jacklyn Stone. You drew up plans for Stone Estates, my son's development, which I now own. If you're available, I'd like to get a revised plan from you. When might be a good time to meet?"

He clears his throat. "I'm sorry, but your son called and asked me, before he was caught in the avalanche, not to conduct business with you."

I hold the phone away from my ear and issue a silent scream at how my son tried to thwart my every move. "That's nonsense. One person can't monopolize your business and stop me from speaking with you."

"He offered me money, if I did what he asked."

I frown. "Did that money materialize?"

"Now that you mention it, no. I haven't seen any money to back up what he said."

"My son Dusty is in Shore Lodge on Cedar Island, and we're not sure if he'll ever get out. Might you be willing to work for me for a fee? I'm interested in changing the plan from a huge home development to one with thirty to forty tiny homes and a dog park."

"Whoa, that's a big change. Dusty didn't say anything about tiny homes."

"No, because he doesn't know about it, and if you speak with him, I'd appreciate you keeping it quiet, until the City approves the permit and building is underway."

"You got it, and I like the idea of smaller homes on the site. It makes sense and these would probably be easier to sell. Better for the environment too."

"I feel the same way."

"I just finished designing a tiny home project, so I'm familiar with the specs and square footage needed for a unit."

I say, "Excellent, and there's another important thing to note. We have an eagle's nest on the property, so we won't be building near it."

"Understood, and I know right where that nest is from walking the property with your son, although he told me to ignore it and draw out plans as if the nest didn't exist."

I grit my teeth and curse Dusty. He was willing to ignore the eagle's nest and build, baby, build, but when things went awry, he turned me into the City for having an eagle's nest on the site. It's clear my vindictive son puts his own needs first, and he's only out for himself.

I say, "I'm scaling down the project in size and cost from what you did for Dusty. Given your expertise, do you think thirty or forty tiny homes will fit on the parcel? We'll bring in sewer, water and electric utilities, of course. But I'll rely on your judgement to tell me what's best. You're the expert, and this project is already getting attention in town. People want homes like this, because they can't afford what's on the market. That's why I'm ditching the big, sprawling mansions to build affordable, smaller homes."

"When you put it that way, I'm in. Send me a deposit of five grand, and I'll work on it and let you know what I come up with. But I have to say, from what I remember, your site could hold more like two hundred tiny homes."

"I'll think about it, but I wanted to build on a smaller scale, so I'd have less financial pressure and the new home owners would feel like it was a special place. I suppose we could have fifty homes, and reserve room for fifty more for potential future development, if the dog park still works, given that. And thank you, I appreciate your willingness to work together, and I look forward to hearing from you. I'll send you the money today."

We say goodbye and I hang up, massaging my temples. I've taken one small step but much more remains to be done. Sitting at the dining table, I transfer the money and drum my fingers on the table. My son broke into my house in a recent home invasion, running toward my study, but I tripped him and tied him up, while my dog Buddy took care of the other intruder. I haven't felt comfortable working in the study since then. At every whisper of a sound, I jerk and jump up, expecting my devious son to appear.

Running a finger across my lips, I wonder where my niece is now. Emily was due to arrive early this afternoon, but when I called her this morning to ask about her favorite foods, I wasn't able to reach her. I hope nothing bad happened. But she's probably busy driving and having a good time, singing to herself with the radio on. There's nothing to worry about, so I'll put it out of my mind.

16

EMILY

Shivering in the room's cool temperature, I hope my cat is warm enough. I stare at the ceiling, trying to figure out a way to buy time. If I sign the forms, they'll go ahead with their plans to give me an experimental drug and cut into me, taking a kidney. I get the feeling Helmet Hair would like to ditch Counter Guy and Fletcher. The weak link is Fletcher, because he signaled regrets about working on this project, so I'll focus on winning him over to my side.

Counter Guy slaps his hands against his thighs and says to Fletcher and Helmet Hair, "A dead cat and a gone girl don't matter in the big picture. The girl is trouble, so let's kill them. I'll lure in the next subject when she checks into the motel."

My stomach sours. Helmet Hair cocks her head, Fletcher furrows his brow.

Helmet Hair says, "But that doesn't line up with our timeline. We need this girl to be the final patient in the study, so we can conduct the analysis and submit the paper before the deadline."

Counter Guy eyes me. "The organ donor gig is lucrative, and her healthy kidney will bring in top dollar. I've got a buyer waiting for it on the dark web. The stupid study doesn't matter."

Breaking out coughing, I say, "Please, don't take my kidney."

Helmet Hair says, "This'll be no problem for you. You'll breeze right through the operation. Your kidney will replace itself, and you'll be fine."

Nathan Fletcher scratches his cheek and looks away.

Counter Guy nods.

Helmet Hair leaves and returns, pushing a rolling cart. She snaps on purple disposable gloves and holds up a long needle. "We'll draw blood before and after the study drug is administered. And we'll confirm your blood type for the organ donation. Because you're a non-smoker, your kidney is in high demand. So, let's get started. Are you ready to sign the consent documents?"

My eyes fix on six empty vials on the rolling tray beside her. My stomach knots. "How do you know I'm a non-smoker? You didn't ask me about it."

Helmet Hair arches an eyebrow. "That's right, we didn't, did we? I just assumed. Why, do you smoke?"

Thinking fast, I lie. "Yes, I smoke two packs a day of unfiltered cigarettes. No one would want my organs."

She tilts her head. "You're lying to me, so stop trying to throw me off. We looked into you before you arrived, and I know you're not a smoker."

My chest tightens at losing a skirmish, but the battle isn't over. "Please, I can't stand the sight of blood. Don't do this."

She says, "Just sign the forms and get it over with."

"I can't sign with my wrists tied up. Cut these off."

She frees my right wrist, and Fletcher puts a clipboard in front of me.

I blow out a breath. "I want to see my cat. If you bring her to me, I'll sign these."

Helmet Hair crosses her arms. "Of course. We'll keep your cat safe if you sign the consent forms."

"Cut off the wrist restraints, bring me my cat, and I'll sign whatever you want. My cat and I need to be together."

Fletcher cuts the restraints and puts a pen in my hand. Helmet Head whispers to Counter Guy, "Prepare the cat for burial."

My heart races, and I reach over and jab the pen into Fletcher's forearm, drawing blood. He yelps, jumps back and holds his arm. Blood seeps out.

My stomach curdles, and I turn away from the sight of fresh wet blood.

Helmet Hair says to him, "Toughen up. Don't whine. Get her signatures."

He clenches his jaw. Blood drips down his arm, and he says, "I need a bandage. Be right back."

He rushes away, and I leap out of bed, but I'm dizzy. The room whirls around. Standing on weak legs and holding on to the bed, I want to run but my body won't cooperate.

Helmet Hair quickly swoops in, latching my wrist to a bed rail. Her dark eyes narrow. "We thought you'd be an easy patient, and one who went along with the program and wouldn't cause any problems. We will pay you. Why are you putting up a fuss? Get over it."

I force a smile and tell lies. "My aunt knows where I am, and she's on her way. She's formidable, and she'll bring the police force down on you and your gang."

Helmet Hair chuckles, along with the others. But then she stops and jerks her head, staring at Counter Guy. "Is any of what she just said true? Did you not vet this subject adequately? If you slipped up, you know what'll happen to you."

Counter Guy cocks his head. "I checked, and it's not my fault. There was no record of her having an aunt. I think she's lying to buy time."

Helmet Hair studies me and says, "He'd better be right, or your head is on the chopping block."

17

NATHAN FLETCHER

I stride to a back room and find a first aid kit, breaking open and running a moist antiseptic pad over the wound on my right forearm. My skin stings, and I wince. The last subject in our research study isn't cooperating, like the others did. I've lost my objectivity as a researcher, and I shouldn't care about what will happen to her, but I do feel sorry for her.

I draw a breath and slowly let it out, trying to slow my racing heart. My forearm throbs, blood oozes out, and I slap on a bandage. I wish I could give the frantic girl her cat and let her go, but I can't. She needs to stay here, so I'll be paid my part for her kidney. I must have her lab results in the study, or I can't submit the paper and my bid for tenure is toast.

I swallow bitter bile, picturing what will happen to Emily if she doesn't cooperate and sign the consent forms.

She'll die, and I hope she realizes that. These fiends are ready to rip out her kidney and let her die after we follow my clinical trial protocol.

A stray thought skitters past, and I cock my head. What if I dropped the clinical study, abandoned my dream of being a tenured professor and ran for freedom with Emily?

I shake my head, check the bandage on my forearm and leave the back room, walking toward the final subject in my study. She'll take the study drug or the placebo and have her kidney removed. My father would have been so ashamed of me, but I don't have it in me to stop. I'm a weak, selfish criminal who is deep in debt, posing as an associate professor.

18

EMILY

Counter Guy steps close, his strong body odor wafting out, and I wrinkle my nose. I've got to get out of this place, and the only person who might realize I'm in trouble and come find me is Mellie, because I said I might call her today. But knowing Mellie, she'll shrug it off and assume I'm busy on my road trip, which turned into a dark nightmarish dance with impending death.

I bite my lower lip and hope my aunt will call and, when I don't pick up the phone or reply to a text, she'll worry. But in this stark, sterile space, I have no sense of how much time has passed since I checked into the motel and dozed on the double bed. I might have been out for hours or days.

Issuing a heavy sigh, I doubt my aunt will bother to track me down. It's been a long time since we saw each other at my parents' memorial service, years ago on a June afternoon, when I'd just graduated from high school. She was the only family member there, and she gave me the biggest hug. Aunt Jacklyn said she understood my not holding a reception after the service, given my complicated mixed feelings about my parents. I bet she offered me her spare bedroom out of a sense of family obligation. She won't look for me, and no one will, so I'd better figure this out on my own.

Looking around, I search for a weapon and a way out. The white walls are bare. Overhead lights casting an eerie glow, and light bulbs emit a high-pitched whine. A faucet drips.

I tilt my head, listening for sounds of traffic from a roadway, or signs of life outside, but all is quiet. This appears to be a soundproofed room in an isolated facility far away from help. The two older people in hospital beds haven't moved, and I hope they're not dead.

I grimace and wish I'd stayed on freeways, instead of listening to Mellie. She was the one who suggested I take a scenic highway and stay at the motel. She said, "You only live once, so why not enjoy yourself and see beautiful sights along the way?"

But during my trip, I was anxious about moving and didn't notice much about my surroundings. I should have been suspicious when she mentioned her idea, because if I step back, it sounds like a scary movie, where a young woman travels alone on a side road. She stops at an older motel late at night, takes the last available room and wakes with her wrist strapped to a hospital bed. They'll operate and take her kidney, leaving her for dead.

My gut knots, and I swallow bitter bile. What a fool I was to fall into their trap. It's my fault. I took a room and was locked in for the night. I thought I'd sleep through the night and leave the next morning, but it's far worse than I could ever have imagined. Suppressing an urge to whimper, I bite my tongue. I will not show them weakness. I'll be tough and find my cat, fleeing for freedom.

Counter Guy grabs the clipboard, puts it under my hand and places a pen between my fingers. He applies pressure, and I resist, but he forces a scribbled fake signature on one page and then another. Leaning in, I snap my teeth, intending to bite him, but he jumps back and hands the clipboard with the signatures to Helmet Hair.

Fletcher parts the curtain and comes in, stepping to my bedside. His eyes flick over me, and a serious look crosses his face. If I had to guess, I'd say he has regrets about being here and forcing people to participate in his clinical trial and to donate organs. He might help me escape.

Helmet Hair shoves the clipboard at Fletcher. "File these forms and keep them for our records. Take photos, in case everything goes downhill and we're arrested. We'll use them to prove our innocence. Now, let's wrap up the research project. After that, we'll remove her kidney."

"While we have her open, let's take a chunk of her

liver," Country Guy says. "There's a lot of demand for kidneys and livers on the dark web. Might as well double our money."

My body goes cold, and I release a high-pitched scream, squirming and trying to free myself. Wrist restraints cut into my skin and stop me from running for my life. "Let me go. Help. Someone help me."

19

NATHAN FLETCHER

Emily squirms on the bed, issuing blood-curdling screams. Hugging the clipboard to my chest, my knees tremble. She's about my age, and her life is just starting to unfold, but she made the mistake of stopping at a motel on a little traveled road. Like others before her, she may die from infections post-surgery, after we leave her to recover on her own.

I wipe my upper lip. If she ends up taking the placebo pill, she'll feel terrible pain during her surgery. Icepicks of guilt stab at my heart. I shouldn't be taking part of this. It isn't right.

Doubts race through my mind, and I frown. I've put my career goals and greed above the needs of the poor people who have had their kidneys ripped from their bodies. I have pretended I didn't know what was happening and looked the other way when donors died.

But I can't fool myself any longer. What we're doing has deadly consequences, and I'm part of the problem. My father would cry if he could see me now.

I sway on my feet, as if standing on the edge of a moral cliff. I could help Emily escape, but that would fail, and we'd both die. They'd take my liver and kidneys and not administer pain medications, just to punish me. Members of this crime ring don't tolerate dissension. When a redheaded middle-aged janitor complained about not being paid enough for working long hours, she disappeared.

Tapping my lower lip, I nod as Emily thrashes and wails. If nothing else, I hope she'll take the pill to possibly calm her anxiety.

I glance at her fake signatures on the two consent forms. Tucking the clipboard under my arm, I stride away, hounded by the howling of my guilty conscience.

My stomach churns with acid. My father would expect me to ignore the consequences and free Emily, but I just can't. The desire to become a tenured professor has made me blind to these horrible crimes.

JACKLYN

In the afternoon, I check the time, close the mystery I'm reading and fidget with my fingers. I have too much energy to sit and wait for my niece to arrive, so I get up and pace the living room floor, mumbling to myself. Buddy opens an eye, watching me from the couch. Opening my hands, I say, "Emily said she'd be here by now. I hope nothing has happened. She's probably fine, but I'll call her."

Pulling my phone from a pocket, I dial my niece Emily's number for the third time in an hour. It rings and rings, but finally, just as I'm about to hang up, someone answers. A man sounds out of breath when he says, "Hello?"

Cocking my head, I say, "Hello, I'm calling my niece. Who is this?"

He whispers, "I can't tell you my name, but Emily is in trouble. You need to get here fast."

My pulse races. "Where is she?"

"In a warehouse by The Gas Station Motel. Bring the police."

"Why? What's wrong?"

"You'll find out soon enough."

I say, "What town is she in? Who are you?"

He hangs up, and I hear a dull dial tone.

My heart pounds in my chest, and I call Irena to ask for help, because she's excellent in a crisis, but she doesn't pick up. I frown, because she always answers and runs to danger. Something must be going on with her, and I hope all is well.

I dial my friend Mercury, and he answers right away. "My niece is in trouble, and a man told me to bring the cops and get there as soon as I can. Will you go with me?"

"Sure, where are we heading?"

"Emily is being held in a warehouse by The Gas Station Motel, but where that is, I have no idea." I grip the phone tight.

"Let me look it up." After a beat, he says, "I see it, but unfortunately, it's two hours away, southeast of here. Given how it's raining, it might take us longer to get there."

I tap a toe. Buddy hops off the couch and trots over, sitting and staring at me. A million thoughts race through my mind. "From what the man said, we need to get there soon to avert disaster. I'll call the FBI agent who helped us when Jack went missing and owed money to a crook."

"Are you sure that's necessary? How sure are you of what you heard?"

"I'm very sure. He sounded like it's a life-or-death situation. He answered Emily's phone, told me she's in trouble and that I needed to get to the building by the motel right away and bring the police."

"Okay, I'll be right over. What was the FBI agent's name?"

"Frankie McNalley. I'll call her now. I need someone to watch Buddy, so I'll ask my neighbor Jenna."

I call Jenna, who lives two doors down, and she agrees to walk Buddy and take care of him until I return. When I call Special Agent Frankie McNalley, she answers right away.

I say, "This is Jacklyn Stone, and I think my niece is caught up in a terrible situation. I called her phone, and a strange man told me she's being held in a warehouse by The Gas Station Motel, southeast of here a few hours. He said Emily's in trouble and to get there fast and bring the police. Would you please look into it and tell the police? Mercury and I are on our way."

Agent McNalley says, "Hold on." She speaks to someone on her end of the line in a low voice, and then says to me, "We've long suspected a crime ring was operating in that area and harvesting organs to sell on the black market, but we haven't been able to prove it. I'll check with my boss, but I'm pretty sure we'll send a team right away, and I might see you there."

I whoosh out a breath. "Thank you for taking this seriously. I appreciate it."

"We'll talk later." She hangs up, and Mercury pulls up outside in his pickup truck. I toss Buddy a dog biscuit, pull on my jacket and run out into the rain.

21

HELMET HAIR

Fletcher leaves with the signed consent forms, and I smile, saying to the man who works at the motel front counter, "Nice work, getting her signatures. Pretty soon we'll carve out a kidney to help a desperate person. We're in the helping business, aren't we?"

He smirks. "Yep, we're in this for altruistic reasons."

I grin. "Wealthy people will pay big bucks for a healthy kidney, and hers will bring top dollar. Tight supply and increasing demand are driving up prices."

Emily, the organ donor wails and whines, pulling on her wrist restraints. She says, "Don't do this. I was on a road trip, and my friend said to stay at the motel. This is Mellie's fault. Let me go."

My gaze meets the counter guy's, because we threatened Mellie, who pointed a deflecting finger at Emily. I work hard for my money, and I disliked Mellie's entitled attitude enough that I was ready to let a doctor carve into her. But she sweet talked her way out of it with a wad a cash and by offering up her friend Emily.

Checking the time, I purse my lips. "The doctor was supposed to be here by now. Wonder what's keeping him?"

Counter Guy shrugs. "Might be the rain, with all the slow drivers."

"Don't get me started on people who drive slow in the rain, creeping along."

He nods. "Yeah, I know."

I roll my eyes. "And the idiots who drive ten miles an hour in snow with bald tires, sliding and skidding on the road. They're a danger to everyone and shouldn't go out if they can't handle the conditions."

Emily says, "This is wrong, what you're doing. You can't trap people and take their organs."

I snort. "We'll pay you, so stop complaining. You need the money, and we want your kidney. It's a business arrangement, and everyone's happy, so settle down."

She glares. "Nothing gives you the right to take advantage of people. I don't want your money. Just cut me loose, and I'll stay quiet."

"Fat chance of that happening. We have a buyer lined up. We'll confirm your blood type and proceed with the operation when the physician arrives. End of discussion."

Tears run down her cheeks. "Mellie pricked my finger

and blotted up blood with a tissue last week when I was asleep. I woke up when she jabbed me. She said she was sleep-walking, but I knew something was weird. I shouldn't have believed her. Let me see my cat."

I cross my arms and say to Counter Guy, "Where's Fletcher?"

22

COUNTER GUY

I frown, wanting to get this operation over and done. The donor is way too loud and putting up too much of a fuss for my liking. Her screaming is giving me a headache. We should've kept her drugged, but Fletcher insisted we get valid signatures on the forms and look how well that worked out. I was the one who saved the day and forced her to sign, but no one thanked me for that.

I swallow, and bitter resentment at how this operation is going bubbles up. I'm in charge, but the other two don't act like it. Because my roots are in this out of the way rural area, they talk down to me. Who cares if Fletcher teaches at a college and she, with the stiff over-hair sprayed hair, is the operations manager? I deserve respect, and I'm going to get it. I'm the crucial part of this scheme. I work at the front desk, lure people into special motel rooms and find buyers on the dark web. Without me, none of this would be possible.

Scratching my stubbled chin, I decide to ask my boss Stanley, who runs the crime ring, for a raise. I deserve it for all I put up with, working with these two idiots. I'll bring it up next time I see him, but right now he's off on a yacht, basking in warmth and relaxing where the sun shines. I'll suggest he promote me while he's at it and move me closer to headquarters in Tacoma.

Helmet Hair claps her hands and says in a loud voice, "Nurses, come in. We're ready to begin."

I say, "It's about time. Let's get this show on the road."

She arches an eyebrow. "Do you have somewhere you have to be that's more important than this?"

I cock my head, picturing a poker game I'll join after I leave. "Maybe I do."

She scoffs. "We're in the middle of farm fields. There's nothing to do. Where would you go? Nowhere fast."

I glower. "You breeze in with your big city attitude and miss what's going on right under your nose. It's not so bad living here."

23

EMILY

My body shudders, imagining horrible horrors ahead. Four white-clad nurses with caps swish through the parted red curtain and stride into the enclosed space, heading for me. My hands tremble. Helmet Hair says, "Hook her up to the machines, so we can monitor her vital signs."

A chill creeps up my spine. Whatever is about to happen is my fault for staying in a motel room that was only accessible through an empty storefront. How stupid was that? When I set out from my hometown, my thoughts were muddled with regrets about moving. But now my mind is crystal clear. I want to discover what's next for me down the road of my life. I don't want to die today or tomorrow or the day after that. I want to live.

My pulse picks up. I'll find my cat, and we'll escape. I'll drive away and start a new life. I'll floor it and get as far away from here as I can. The only question I have is how to accomplish that.

A nurse wearing bright red lipstick approaches me with a blood pressure cuff. She smiles, and her pointed canine teeth stand out, looking chiseled, as if she's ready to bite into flesh. I grimace and move away from her.

She looks over at Helmet Hair. "Most of the other patients went along with the program. What's different about this one?"

Helmet Hair scowls. "We're not sure. She was selected for the study, but now I'm questioning that decision. She's defiant." She says to me, "Did you have a difficult childhood?"

I press my lips together. I won't tell them about my past. Secrets are meant to be kept close, not bandied about for social currency. That's what I told Mellie when she pressed me about my odd upbringing in a household with two musicians who worked nights and taught music lessons during the day in our house.

Helmet Hair shakes a raised bedrail until it rattles. Her face is flushed, and I know the signs of barely suppressed anger from growing up with a parent who kept a soup pot of aggression simmering on the back burner of life at all times.

I avert my eyes from her gaze, because I know from experience that a direct confrontation with someone like that, who fuels the fires of resentment burning within, is destined to fail. Get along to get along, I tell myself, and watch for a crack in their system. Be ready to leap out of bed and run when the moment is right. I'll find my cat, flee to a place far away and start a new life, beyond their twisted reach.

Chisel Tooth wraps a blood pressure cuff around my bicep. A nurse with short gray hair attempts to put sticky electrodes on my legs, but I move them away. With a frown, she says, "She keeps moving. Help hold her down, so I can get this done."

Counter Guy comes over, placing his sweaty hands on my flesh. I kick my legs, and he swears. Fletcher comes in, eyes darting around the room, as if he wants to run from this madness as much as I do.

Helmet Hair says to Fletcher, "Get in here and help. Keep her legs still, so we can start. We're on a tight deadline, and the kidney has to be on a plane soon."

Pairs of strong hands grasp my legs, pinning them to the bed. The gray-haired nurse places round stickers with attached wires on my legs. She says, "Now for the head, torso and arms."

"Stop," I scream. "Let me walk out the door with my cat, and I won't report you or tell anyone about this terrible experiment on innocent people. I'll keep it a secret for the rest of my life, I swear I will. Just let me go, along with the two old people in beds over there."

Counter Guy says, "It sounds like she's reached the stage of bargaining."

Helmet Hair nods. "First, anger. Then bargaining, and

later comes acceptance." She stares at me with cold dark eyes. "Give in and accept your fate. You don't have any control. Besides, you might survive the kidney donation. Some of our volunteers do, despite the lack of post-op support, which keeps our costs down. Be optimistic going into the operation. That'll help your outcome."

I glare. "You're deluding yourselves. I'm not a volunteer. You drugged me and forced me to sign away my rights."

A nurse says, "Hold her head down, so she won't thrash."

Fletcher grips my head with warm hands.

Gray Hair lifts a sensor from a cart and comes toward me, but I shake my head and break free of Fletcher's hands, so she can't do her job. My heart races, and I'm out of breath from the effort of fighting them.

Helmet Hair strides over. "Here, let me show you how to do it."

Strong fingers grip my scalp, holding it in place like a vise, and her sharp fingernails dig into my skull. I wince at stabbing pains, and a pounding headache throbs. Realizing fighting hasn't worked, I give in and relax my tense muscles, resting my weary head on a pillow. I wish someone would come in and stop these vicious violators, and I'd run out, racing away. How little I valued and appreciated my small life before, but now every moment I've lived is filled with meaning.

Helmet Hair's stale coffee breath blows in my face, and

I breathe through my mouth, so as not to smell it. She says, "This is how to do it. Eventually, the subject gives up. You just have to overpower them long enough."

I suppress a groan and tell myself to conserve my energy and wait for an opening to attempt to escape. They're in a hurry to wrap up their research project, so they might make mistakes. I'll play along and pounce on an opportunity when it presents itself.

I let my limbs go limp, so they'll think I don't pose a threat, and say, "Fine, do what you want. I don't care. I was fired. I couldn't find a job and had to leave my hometown. I'm a loser, so go ahead and gather your data. Take my kidney and get it over with. The sooner the better. But before I die, I'd like to say goodbye to my sweet cat."

24

———

NATHAN FLETCHER

Clenching my jaw, I wish I could do more to help Emily. Most of us in this room are motivated by money, but Emily doesn't seem obsessed with it. She's unemployed and has little in her bank account, but she'd rather be free than receive payment for an organ donation.

I swallow hard, feeling unsettled. My conscience took over when I left the room and wrestled me down, urging me to answer Emily's ringing phone. I told whoever called to come quick, but we're far from anywhere. It'll take a while for help to arrive, and even if it does, we have local police officers on our payroll.

Licking my dry lips, I mull over what to do. I could slip out the door and avoid getting arrested. But I'm a fish on a line, hooked by the bait of observing this last subject in the study complete the protocol. I've waited eleven months for this day and salivated at the idea of analyzing the results and writing the research paper. The short amount of time remaining to crunch the data is ridiculous. If I can take the data with me, before authorities arrive. I could publish it later in a different journal. I wouldn't need to run it past she-who-thinks-she-is-queen, her with the helmet of hair, that way.

Emily looks directly into my eyes, and something about her strength speaks to me. She's not beaten down, like many others who have passed through this room, having hit rock bottom. Drawing a breath, I wonder how I'd feel if I were the one about to be cut open on an operating room table. Not as calm as her, I'm sure.

Heaving a sigh and thinking of how my father would see all this, I know I must toss my clinical study aside. I just can't publish data from a study when subjects were forced to comply. I can't let them operate on Emily without her consent. Dad would want me to shut down the crime ring. I've got to stop this at all costs.

Emily says, "I want to see my cat."

My forearm throbs where she stabbed it, but I nod. She wants her cat, and it's one thing I can do to make her feel better about this ugly situation. I'll start with a small act of kindness, reuniting her with her cat, while I consider diving into deeper waters and risking my life.

25

JACKLYN

Rain drums down on the car roof, and the wiper blades complain about their tedious journey across the windshield, swishing back and forth. Mercury clenches his jaw and trains his eyes on the wet road ahead as he drives. He says, "Another hour to go is my best guess. What do you think?"

"That sounds about right. I hope this doesn't turn out to be a waste of time, chasing down a lead that could be someone's idea of a practical joke. But deep down, I suspect something serious happened to delay my niece. The man who answered her phone sounded scared. The FBI suspects an organ harvesting crime ring is operating in the area. What if they're going to cut Emily open?"

He cringes. "That'd be awful. I'd hate to be used as an unwilling organ donor. I can't think of a worse way to die."

I shudder. "I hope we won't be too late. Poor Emily,

after all she's been through. Her parents died in a car crash the day she graduated from high school, and a drunk driver killed them."

Mercury sighs, shaking his head. "That's rough. The poor kid."

"It turned out her parents took out a reverse mortgage on their house, and there was nothing left for Emily after they died. No home, no money to fall back on, but she does have a therapy cat, because she gets anxious at times."

"Don't we all?"

I nod. "Without Buddy, the last year would've been much more difficult after Albert died, so I can understand having a therapy animal."

My phone rings, and I glance at the screen, suspecting it's another spam caller. Seeing it's Jenna, I answer. "Hi, how's Buddy?"

"I'm sorry, but he got out."

My jaw drops. My pulse pounds. "What?"

Jenna says, "He's racing around in front of the house and won't come when I call. What should I do? He looks like he's having a good time, but it's dangerous with cars coming down the road."

I clap a hand to my chest, and tears spring to my eyes. "Run in the kitchen and grab the box of dog biscuits on the counter and run outside, yelling, 'Buddy, treat! Treat!' Wave one around and call his name in a high-pitched voice. Sound happy and excited, and he should come right away. I hope it'll work."

"I'll try it." She hangs up, and the line goes dead.

I clench my hands. "Good grief, as if we don't have enough going on, now this."

Mercury says, "Fill me in. What was that about?"

I relay the news to him and say, "I hope she'll be able to bring him back inside before a car drives down the road. I don't want to lose that sweet pup."

He grunts. "Fortunately, there's not much traffic down your street. He's a good dog. I hope he'll be okay."

I wipe my palms on my pants. "I hope so too."

26

EMILY

Nurses attach round stickers with electrodes to my forehead and arms, and I practice slow breathing, in and out, waiting and watching for a chance to run. I picture myself holding my cat, and my pulse slows. No one responded to my request to see my cat, and I'll repeat it, but not yet. I'll bide my time.

Imagining ruining their evil experiment, I smile but wipe it away. Helmet Hair's back is turned to me, and she and Counter Guy talk in hushed voices. I can't hear what they're saying, but Counter Guy nods and leaves. I follow his movements as he strides to a door marked 'Exit.' He yanks it open and hurries out.

My chest feels light and I breathe easier, because now I know a way out.

Helmet Hair marches over to the door, pulls a metal key from her shirt pocket and inserts it in the lock, turning it. The lock snicks shut, and she removes the key, slipping it in the front pocket of her red shirt.

She meets my gaze, but I glance away, not wanting her to suspect I'm planning my exit. A nurse unties my hospital gown and the fabric slips down in front, exposing my bare chest. I gasp and hunch over, drawing my shoulders together. "You could at least grant me some privacy and respect."

Everyone in the room erupts in laughter. I pull my elbows close to my chest in a last-ditch effort at modesty and say in a loud voice, "I want my cat. You've screwed with me long enough and messed with my rights. Bring her to me and put her on my lap."

Fletcher says, "I'll get the cat." He steps out and turns right, disappearing behind a red curtain and moving with hurried footsteps in a different direction than Counter Guy went. Cool air blows past, and when a door slams shut, I realize there must be two ways out of this wretched place. Minutes pass, and I breathe slowly, weaving a vision in my mind of running out.

A door to my right creaks open, and a breeze blows past, carrying a whiff of fresh air, and I nod, secure in the knowledge that the door on my right leads directly outside. I hope my cat wasn't stranded in the rain while I was stuck in this wretched room.

Fletcher strides to the bed, holding a cat carrier with my meowing tabby cat inside. He sets the cat carrier gently on my lap, and my throat grows tight. In a tearclogged voice, I say to my cat, "Julep, I'm sorry this happened. I should've protected you better."

Silence fills the room, and I study the tiger-stripe markings on my cat to see if she's okay and make sure they didn't switch her with another feline while I was asleep. She's my cat, that's for sure, and I break down in tears, weeping for my idiotic move of taking a room in a strange motel under questionable circumstances. I should've jumped in my car and kept driving, despite my fatigue.

Fletcher stands tall, observing me from a few feet away. He takes notes on a device and nods to himself. I doubt I'll get any help from him, given how I jabbed his arm and how much he wants to publish the study results to get tenure at a university.

I make a face and remove him from my list of potential helpers for my flight to freedom. Turning on the tears, I bend over the cat crate and look up, saying to Helmet Hair, "Please help me. Take off the restraints from my wrists, so I can open the crate and hold my cat. She's traumatized and needs me."

A nurse in her late twenties with long brown hair pulled back in a ponytail says, "Let her hold her cat. Depriving her of being with her therapy cat isn't right. We shouldn't do that."

Helmet Hair's voice cuts through the beeping machines at my bedside. "We do this work for the sake of science and to help others. Remember that. If anything happening in this room bothers you, walk away and don't come back to work. You have a choice. If you say anything, we'll track you down, and you'll disappear."

I cock my head and bite back a complaint about how I'm the only one in the room without choices. "Please," I say in a trembling voice, "remove the restraints. I'll be good. You can trust me. I've calmed down, and I understand how important this project is to you. I'll support your efforts."

Helmet eyes me, and her gaze flicks around the room. She shrugs. "Fine, release her but keep a close watch. We don't want her escaping when we least expect it. And I'll remind you all one last time. We can't jeopardize our chances of publishing these results in a peer-reviewed journal, and the deadline for submission is tomorrow morning at eight o'clock."

Fletcher scratches the back of his neck. "I thought the deadline was eleven tomorrow morning. I'll never make it if it's earlier in the day. I need time to analyze the results and write the abstract. It's cutting it ridiculously close as it is."

Helmet Hair slams her fist on the bedrail, and I flinch. My cat meows. Fletcher's head jerks.

Helmet says, "You idiot. No wonder you don't have tenure. I'm right, and you're wrong. The deadline is eight tomorrow morning, but you must send me the article by midnight tonight, so I have time to review and approve it before you submit it."

His jaw tightens, and a vein throbs in his forehead.

He's fiercely unhappy with Helmet Hair, and despite my hurting him, he's moved up on my list as a candidate to help me slip out and leave this room behind.

Fletcher pulls out a knife and cuts a zip tie around my wrist attached to a railing. I move to grab the knife, but my fingers are numb. He folds the blade, slips it back in his pocket and catches my gaze, giving me a subtle nod.

My fingers tingle, and I shake out my hands to get blood flowing. I coo to my cat, open the crate door and take her out, holding a red leash attached to her harness. She rests her paws and warm furry body on my chest, and a nurse frowns. "Be careful. Don't let the cat pull off the sensors. We need the data."

Helmet Hair says, "That's right. Everything we do is for science."

Fletcher coughs into his hand. "And for money."

Two old folks doze in their beds, and I wonder if their organs will be harvested and sold to the highest bidder. Biting my lower lip, I feel like an idiot, like Mellie tells me. I never told her how much that hurt my feelings, and I'll make sure any future friends will support me, not hurt me.

A memory of my mother's voice rings in my ears. Pay attention, she'd harp, then she'd throw up her hands and walk out of the room, leaving me on my own in grade school. Tears dripped down, wetting the paper, and numbers swam before my eyes. Memories flash through my mind of when I was in second grade and nervous about being in class with a boy who bullied me, yanking on my ponytail. When I told my parents, they laughed and said he liked me. I pointed to a patch of missing hair on my scalp, and they smiled, waving my pain away. That's when I knew I was on my own, and I couldn't trust adults to protect me. Now it feels like I'm right back there, alone, and in grade school.

The cat purrs, kneading my chest with her paws, and I pet her head, scratching behind her ears. At least if we end up dead, we'll be together.

27

JACKLYN

While Mercury drives, I call Jenna, and she says, "Buddy's fine. He came inside, and he's sitting by me on the couch." Releasing a relieved sigh, I say, "Oh, thank goodness. I'm glad he's safe and inside."

"I've got to leave, but I'll check on him later. Detectives asked me to come in and answer questions about how Kirk embezzled money from employers."

I bite my lip. "Oh, dear. Did you know he was doing that?"

"No, I had no idea, even though we were married. I trusted him completely and thought we told each other everything, until this came out of the blue."

"Do you think it was all his ex-wife's fault?"

"Zoila might've been the instigator and gotten him started years ago, but he made the choice to take money before she reappeared in our lives and moved next door. Listen, I've got to go, but I'll check on Buddy later."

I say, "Remember to give Buddy his second dinner, and thanks for doing this."

"You bet. That's what friends and neighbors are for."

We hang up, and Mercury says, keeping his eyes on the road, "Sounds like all is well at home?"

"Yes, Buddy is safe inside, and Jenna is leaving to talk to detectives about her husband's case. Or, rather, her soon to be ex-husband's case."

Mercury shakes his head. "You've sure had some drama going on down the block. That was a strange situation, with Kirk's ex-wife living next door to him and his new wife."

"That didn't work out well. Living right next door to each other was crazy, and it's too bad Zoila got away. Who knows where she is now. She's probably preying on some poor soul in another town."

He tugs on his mustache. "She's a black widow. I feel sorry for whoever gets involved with her next."

I wave a hand in front of my face. "Good riddance to Zoila. I think I'll call Irena to see how she's doing."

He shrugs. "Fine with me. We've still got a ways to go."

When Irena picks up, I say, "Is everything okay? I called you, and you didn't answer before."

Her boat's engine rumbles in the background. In a tense voice, she says, "Kelly fell off a dirt bike. She's pretty banged up, but it doesn't sound like anything's broken. I'm on my way to see her on Grand Island, and I'll take her to the walk-in clinic in Friday Harbor."

Looking out into the late afternoon gloom, I say, "Is the clinic open?"

"It's open twenty-four-seven. Got to go."

I hang up and whoosh out a breath. "That beats everything."

Mercury glances over. "What happened?"

"Kelly fell off a dirt bike, which Irena told her not to do. She was afraid something like this might happen. She's headed to Grand Island, and she'll take her to the walk-in clinic on San Juan Island."

"Good thing Irena has a fast boat and knows what she's doing on the water."

"It is. I have a feeling Kelly's going to get an earful from her mother about this. It's not easy, parenting a teenager."

He hunches over the wheel, staring at the road. "I don't know if your son will ever grow out of acting like a teenager, but who knows, maybe being at Shore Lodge will help him grow up."

Rain pelts down on the windshield, and wipers groan, swishing back and forth. With a sigh, I say, "Yes, with him it's me, me, me, all the time. I've given up hope that he'll ever grow up. He's who he is, distilled into a selfish spirit. But I do wonder how things are going for him at Shore Lodge."

28

———

DUSTY

Hunched over in a wheelchair, I grip the armrests and frown at an aide striding down a hall, as I reflect how my mother admitted me to Shore Lodge. Veins stand out in my arms, and I was once a strong man from building houses. But when an avalanche buried me, it sapped my strength. Nurse Wright says I'm lucky that I survived, but when I draw a breath, my lungs hurt. I can barely take two steps while leaning on a walker.

When an aide parked me near the nursing station, where I now sit, she said, "You'd better be good. We'll let you go in the dayroom when you prove we can trust you."

I wanted to dole out a snarky retort, but I couldn't form the words. Nurse Wright and her staff treat me like a child, all because I threw a fit and broke the television when my mother visited. They have a new one mounted on the wall, and I need to get back in the dayroom to teach Nurse Wright and her crew a crucial lesson. Don't talk down to Dusty Stone.

An older resident with frizzy blond hair sits in a plastic chair in the hall, six feet away from me. She tugs on wrist restraints and screeches at the top of her lungs, sounding like a seagull. Occasionally, she breaks out into song in a wavering, high-pitched, grating voice, singing about a husband gone wrong. Just being near her gives me a pounding headache.

Nurse Wright stands at the nursing station and taps a pen against the counter. "Mrs. Skidmore, that's enough."

But Mrs. Skidmore says in a singsong voice, "He left one day when I was doing laundry. The lure of the mistress was strong, but he should have looked away. Instead, I ended up here, tied to a chair."

I cock my head and watch her carefully, because although she appears crazy at a glance, I suspect she's telling the truth and talking about something that happened. Goosebumps prick my arms. Nurse Wright and Dr. Henderson, the head boss, might keep me here under the guise of my requiring additional treatment, but in reality, they're filling beds for profit and to line their pockets.

My skull throbs. I put my head in my hands and moan. Mrs. Skidmore has a right to sing and talk and voice her opinions, but I wish I wasn't parked near her. I'll have to get back in Nurse Wright's graces, so I can escape to the dayroom, where residents sleep in recliners, and a television drones all day.

Nurse Wright comes over and says to Mrs. Skidmore, "Let's have some quiet for a while. Take a break and rest your voice."

Mrs. Skidmore says in a raspy voice, "I want an ice bath."

"Not yet. Maybe later today."

An older woman walks by, slippers slapping on the floor. She adjusts her red bird's nest of a wig and says, "Be good, Dusty, for your mother's sake. Don't break our TV again."

I grit my teeth. Her words egg me on, making me want to smash the television a second time. No one tells me what to do. That's why I've always worked for myself, and my father supported that idea, giving me money behind Mom's back.

Two gray-haired women with braids down their backs and wearing matching green cardigan sweaters nod to me and make their way toward the day room. When my mother visited me, she spoke with the Twin Cardigans and the woman with the red wig. She must have made friends with them during her stay here, after I admitted her. I'd like to strangle Mom's friends for acting like life is fine in a locked psych ward, where windows don't open, and we can't go outside. Mom wouldn't understand how I feel.

Nurse Wright turns her attention to me. "Dusty, in a

few days, we'll give you the privilege of TV time in the dayroom. That is, if you behave. And that's a big if."

I groan, covering my face with my hands. I don't want TV time, like a toddler. I want to walk and talk and feed myself and chew real food. I want to breathe fresh air. I want to stay in my cabin, where I used to live. I hope my mother paid rent on the cabin to hold it for when I recover and get out. She'd better have done that.

I grab the walker a physical therapist left me and pull myself up to standing. My muscles twitch. My legs shake. My arms tremble. I'm a weakling in a man's body, and it's my mother's fault for making me venture into the mountains, ignoring avalanche warnings. The burden of blame for everything that's gone wrong in my life rests squarely on her shoulders.

An aide passes by, staying three feet away. She flicks a gaze full of fear my way and turns to look ahead. The staff steer clear of me, ever since I blew my stack at Mom when she was here. It took them a week to replace the television, and everyone frowned at me, but I'm used to being a pariah. Just let them try being an uncoordinated tall kid with freckles, before I grew into my body. The name Dusty Stone, my mother's choice, made me a target for teasing. Again, it's her fault.

A brown-eyed middle-aged aide in white approaches, carrying a dinner tray of what looks like pablum and porridge. "Dinner, Mr. Stone. We have corn chowder tonight and oatmeal for dessert. No forks for you, after you tried to attack an aide last week. She left and never came back to work. We don't want that to happen again, do we?"

She smiles, but her lips quiver, and I'm pleased to see I make her nervous. It's the only power I have, locked inside Shore Lodge and not able to talk or walk.

"Here's your spoon." She hands it to me.

I take it with trembling fingers. Watching her hurry away, I vow to recover my abilities and get out of here. I'll prove that Nurse Wright was wrong when she told me this was my new home. I won't stay stuck behind these sterile walls, and I won't grow old here. If anyone can come back from defeat, it's me, because I'm made of stone.

29

EMILY

Nurses move around the bed with purpose, pushing buttons on beeping machines with brightly lit displays. A gray-haired nurse attaches two sensors to my chest and says in a soft voice, "After this patient, I'm hopping on a plane to Tahiti and never coming back." My chest tightens, picturing my dead body and my cat's buried in a field where no one will find our remains.

Running a trembling hand over my purring cat, I plot our escape and watch and wait. I say, "I have a headache. Could I have a pain reliever?"

Helmet Hair says, "Funny you should mention that. The next step in the protocol, after we draw blood to establish baseline levels, is to administer a pill and monitor you for negative reactions."

I cringe. "No, I don't want to be in your experiment. Sorry I brought it up."

Fletcher looks up from his notes. "Don't worry. We'll take good care of you."

Something in his eyes and tone of voice convey warmth along with worry, giving me courage.

Helmet Hair smirks. "That's right, we'll be good to you for as long as the ride lasts."

"Could I have a glass of water? My throat is dry."

She says, "You'll have to wait. First, we'll draw your blood and get that checked off the list."

Picturing a needle poking into my skin, I shudder. My cat looks up and rubs her head against me. "Is there any way we can skip that part of the experiment? I faint at the sight of blood, and I don't like needles."

Helmet Hair shakes her head. "Absolutely not. Now hold out your right arm and relax. Nurse, move in and draw her blood. This won't hurt a bit."

Chisel Tooth rolls over a cart with empty vials. She smiles and her sharp canine teeth distract me as she taps my right arm with a gloved finger and slides a needle into my arm. I look away and feel light headed, but comfort comes from a warm furry creature on my lap giving unconditional love. Blowing out a breath, I realize the nurse didn't gouge me and I didn't yelp, like I always do, so that's the first thing that's gone right today.

A few minutes later, Chisel Tooth says in a chipper voice, "We're finished."

I don't look to see how many vials she filled. If I saw them, I might retch and make a mess, diminishing my meager chances of slipping out the door. I remind myself to act compliant, so they'll relax and forget to monitor me closely.

Helmet Hair holds out a large, white round tablet and a cup of water. "Take this pill and swallow it in one gulp. We'll stay with you to monitor how you feel."

"I can't. The pill is too big. I'll cough it up. I'll choke."

She glares. "Patient compliance is critical. Swallow the pill and don't make a fuss about it. We must follow the clinical trial protocol."

She hands the white disc to me, but at the last minute, I turn my head away, and the pill falls to the floor, rolling away.

Helmet Hair puts her hands on her hips, frowning. "Look what you've done. Fletcher, pick it up. We don't have the time to buy more. She's the last patient in the study, and after this, we're finished gathering data."

Fletcher retrieves the pill and holds it in the air. "That's right. Enrollment is closed. When we have her results, I'll run the statistical analysis and write up the report."

But a cloud of concern passes over his face, and he looks down, studying the white linoleum floor. "The trouble is, I normally have six months to perform the analysis and write the report. This is short notice, and I want to do a good job."

Helmet Hair crosses her arms. "Get over yourself and do it. Don't whimper and whine."

Counter Man breezes in through the door directly in front of me and rushes to my bedside. With a smile, he whispers to Helmet Hair, "It's all set. We'll bury her out back with the others, if she dies after we harvest her kidney. No one will find her body."

A chill runs up my spine, and I pet my cat. I don't want to die, not today or tomorrow or the day after that. I want to live and find a job and make new friends. I want a happy life with my cat. I've got to find a way out of this and survive.

30

EMILY

Fletcher dusts off the white pill on his khaki pants, and his forehead glistens with a sheen of sweat. He holds up the pill with a trembling hand. "You need to take this now, given our time constraints. Dawdling doesn't benefit anyone."

I tilt my head, studying him closely, because Fletcher has changed since he came back into the room. His Adam's apple bobs up and down. Whatever happened when he left the room made him nervous. I can only hope it'll somehow benefit my cause, so I can get out of this alive, with all my organs intact.

Nurses gather around, gripping my shoulders and holding me down. I grit my teeth. Escaping with this many people around me is highly unlikely, but I won't give up. For some strange reason, a memory was stirred from when I lost my job as a waitress.

I was in the walk-in freezer eating a piece of cheese-cake one afternoon at the Purple Pickle Deli and hiding from the noisy restaurant. My boss flung open the freezer door and motioned me out. My fingers were damp and sticky with cheesecake, and she pointed to the back door, saying I was fired. I apologized, and my cheeks blazed with heat, but she didn't change her mind. I'd taken too long to serve a table for two a club sandwich and a Reuben. Wiping my fingers on a dish towel, I grabbed my purse and hurried outside, vowing never to tell my parents about the mortifying incident.

Walking home, I knew what I'd done was wrong, which made it ten times worse. I passed a jewelry store and glanced inside, where all appeared quiet. Forcing myself to enter the store, I padded along on thick carpet, going up to an older man working at the counter. I asked if they might have a job open. He smiled, adjusted his glasses and asked if I was meticulous with details and didn't mind polishing silver. I grinned and said yes, and that became my best job ever until the day the store was sold.

That night, my parents came home from playing a concert. Mom set down her violin on a chair by the music stand in the living room, where she gave lessons, and students sawed away on strings. Dad left his trumpet case by the front door and poured a scotch straight up, not looking at me and disappearing into the den.

Mom stared at me and sighed, shaking her head.

Beverly was my mom, but you'd never know it. We didn't look alike, and she had a temper like a soda bottle shook up before it was opened.

She said, "I heard you were fired at the Purple Pickle. What are we going to do with you? I recommended you for the job at the deli and look what you did. Word got out about you stuffing your mouth in the deep freeze in back. I doubt you'll get another job in this town. How are you going to pay us rent?"

She turned her back on me and walked away. I blurted out, "But I got another job already. I'm working at Miller's Jewelry Store. I can still pay the forty dollars a month for room and board."

Her eyebrows shot up. "Believing you gets more and more difficult. Go to bed."

I swallowed a lump in my throat, because it was my birthday, but my parents forgot. I went in the kitchen, opened the freezer and dug out two scoops of chocolate chunk ice cream, plopping them into a bowl. I sat in front of the television in the living room watching a movie I'd seen many times featuring a singing red-headed mermaid. A cold spoonful of delicious creamy chocolate ice cream floated down the back of my throat, and I smiled.

Mom marched in with a scowl on her face and flicked off the television. She stood in front of me, glowering. "What's wrong with you? Can't you do one simple thing I tell you? Go to bed."

My hands trembled, and my pulse pounded in my ears. I jumped off the couch, and the ice cream bowl went flying onto the floor. I ran for the safety of my room, where I'd screwed in a hook and eye latch, and cowered behind the door, hiding from my mother's wrath.

Mom pounded on the door, banging her hip against it. Tears streamed down my cheeks and I braced against the door to keep her out. My pulse raced, my palms were cold, and I waited for what would come next. This time though, Mom said, "Fine, hide in there tonight, but tomorrow's another day."

The next morning, I grabbed my school backpack and crept down the stairs. My pulse picked up with each step. All I had to do was slip outside and get to school before my mom saw me. I opened the front door, inhaled cool fresh air and breathed a sigh of relief, but a sudden motion to my right caught my attention.

Mom slapped the side of my head, making my ears ring. I ran to school and told my teacher what happened, but my mother was persuasive and convinced people she was a fabulous, caring mother.

From the day I was fired from the Purple Pickle Deli, Mom harbored a deep disappointment in me that lingered until the day she and Dad died in a car accident. They were driving home from a special dinner without me, celebrating my high school graduation. Before they got in the car to go out and eat, leaving me home alone,

Mom said, "It's high time you moved out and rented a room somewhere else. I expect to see you gone in a week."

Helmet Hair's gruff voice brings me back to the present. "Swallow the darned pill. Don't fool around, just gulp it down. We're on a tight time schedule. We have to deliver the kidney tonight, or we won't get paid."

31

IRENA

I dock my boat near Tex's waterfront home. Running up a road to her house, I worry about Kelly falling off a dirt bike and knock on the door, slipping inside.

Tex looks up from an armchair, where she's reading a book by the fire. She nods, "Welcome. We're glad to see you."

My daughter sits up on the sofa. "Mom, you came. You didn't have to. I'm fine."

I hurry over and sit beside her, examining her scraped hands. "What were you thinking, getting on a dirt bike, when I expressly told you not to?"

My daughter crosses her arms. "Mom, I'm old enough to do what I want."

A chill sweeps over me, and I shudder at her defiance. I must be calm and set an example for my thirteen-year-old daughter. I inhale a slow breath and let it out, counting to five.

"Besides," Kelly says, opening her cut, scraped hands, "Tex said I could."

My mouth falls open. Tex, our family friend and my silent but vocal investor in my rescue boat business, is hosting my daughter in her home, but this feels like overstepping. Staring at Tex, I say, "Is this true?"

Tex shrugs. "It's true I told Kelly she could go. I didn't want her to be left out and ostracized. Why should she be the only one not riding a dirt bike on trails?"

My heart thumps, and I rest my hands on my hips, considering the wild things I did when I was Kelly's age, like climbing up steep cliffs jutting over the water with my friends. But I don't want her to take the risks I did. I say, "It seems really risky to me, so I'd like her to wait until she's older, like when she's sixteen."

Tex nods, and Kelly sighs, saying, "Fine, I'll wait a year or two. It hurt when I fell off the bike."

I wrap my arms around her, giving her a hug, and she leans into me. Pulling away, I examine her injuries. I say, "We'll go to Friday Harbor to the walk-in clinic right now to get you checked out by a doctor."

She moans. "Mom, I'm fine. I'm scraped up is all."

Tex says, "Whatever you think is best. You're her mother."

I nod and remind myself we're not competing for

Kelly's love. "Tex, we'll be back as soon as we can. I don't want to keep you up late. We'll let ourselves in."

She waves a hand in front of her face. "I'll be up, so don't worry about it. I'd like to hear what the doctors say."

Kelly whines, running a scraped hand over her forehead. "I'm fine. We don't need to go."

I stand and hold out a hand to my daughter. "Let's go."

She gets up. "I don't think I need to, but I'll do it to make you happy."

We say goodbye to Tex and walk down the road in the dark. I match my stride to my daughter's slower pace. She limps along and moves ahead, but groans as she boards my boat. When the engine is warmed up, I release the dock lines, which is normally Kelly's job, and pull in the fenders. I push on the throttle, and we take off, racing across dark water lit by a half-moon. The wind blows, clouds overhead scud past, and it's a beautiful evening, despite the drama.

Swallowing hard, I hope I'm doing the right thing by allowing my daughter to live on Grand Island to attend school. Her father and I would rather have her in Millersville, but we don't want her tortured by gossiping teens who whipped up rumors.

Kelly says, "I didn't want to mention it, because I thought it would make you worry, but my head hurts."

I bite back bitter words about her not following my orders and say in a calm, clear voice, "We'll get it checked out. Thanks for telling me. I love you, hon."

"Love you too, Mom."

32

EMILY

I take the pill from Fletcher's trembling hand and study the flat white round pill, considering what to do. Counter Guy, Fletcher, Helmet Hair and four nurses watch me, standing in front of a backdrop of a flimsy red fabric curtain. Counter Guy stands close to me, his clothes giving off odors of fresh-dug dirt, dry leaves and tractor oil. I wince and vow to avoid the fate of being buried out back.

My mind races, and I pat my cat's back, thinking fast. People died in this room, leaving blood on the hands of Counter Guy, Helmet Hair, Fletcher, and the nurses helping them. Given Fletcher's furrowed eyebrows and heavy sighs when organ harvesting is mentioned, he seems burdened with regrets. As far as I'm concerned, he's guilty for not stopping their plans to take my kidney. He's looking out for his clinical trial, and he only cares about getting published.

Seconds fly by, and I tighten my grip on my cat's harness, searching for a distraction. Helmet Hair fidgets with her fingers. Counter Guy frowns. Fletcher pulls out a gold stopwatch from his pocket, holding it in his hands. The nurses step to the side, whispering to each other.

Across the room, a grizzled older man in a hospital bed opens his eyes and stares at me. I blink, and he points to me and then toward the door Fletcher must have gone through to get my cat.

I flex my leg muscles, preparing to run. My cat purrs on my lap. Gripping the pill and the cup of water, my palms grow moist.

The old man issues a feeble moan. No one reacts.

"Time's up," Counter Guy says, frowning. "Get on with it. I've got to get back to the motel. Customers need to check in."

Fletcher gives me a slight nod. "Go ahead. Gulp it down."

Helmet Hair says in a harsh voice, "Enough already. Swallow the pill. Or we'll have to administer it rectally, which I'm sure you wouldn't want."

I move the pill toward my mouth to buy a few more seconds.

The gray-haired man moans and waves his hands in the air. "Help. Come help my wife. I can't tell if she's breathing."

They all turn and stare in his direction. My heart races, and I drop the water and pill on the floor. Ripping off round sensors, I hold the cat and slip out of bed, hurrying past them and rushing out the door. I don't have much time, and I've got to get away.

Opening a door and running out, I lock the door behind me and step into what feels like a dark enclosed massive space. Cold air blows in my face from an overhead fan. Shaking with fear, I stumble ahead, clutching my cat to my chest.

33

JACKLYN

Drumming my fingers on the seat, I say, "Emily must be scared out of her mind. Do you think the FBI's right, that people are harvesting organs?"

"We should be there in ten minutes," Mercury says, gripping the wheel. "And where ever there's money to be made, crooks will swoop in and take advantage of people. So, sadly, yes, I suspect what the FBI said is right."

I clasp my hands together. "I hope we can get there in time."

He reaches over, patting my arm. "We'll let the FBI handle it. They're the experts."

"If we're first on the scene, we'll have to do something." I eye him carefully. "You're strong. You have a background you don't talk about. Don't you have some ninja skills hidden up your sleeve?"

He nods. "Fine, point taken. I have zip ties in the glove compartment, so pull those out. Can you heft the tire iron?"

I grin. "Of course. I tossed bags of peat moss in the back of pickups for my garden store, so that won't pose a problem."

He smiles. "Let's agree on a plan, in case we get there before the cops do. You'll sashay inside, pretending to be an innocent aunt looking for her niece, but what they don't know is you have a tire iron tucked under your coat, and you're ready to hit them on the head."

"Sure," I say, pulse racing. "I'll do whatever I have to. I hope they're not operating on her. What're you going to do while I distract them?"

"Don't worry about my part. I'll be skulking around, then I'll join you inside."

I release a tight breath. "It's the best we can come up with on short notice, so this will have to work."

He's quiet for a beat. "This could be very tricky. These thugs could be armed and dangerous, if what we suspect is true."

I swallow, and my throat is dry. "She's family and has no one else to look out for her. I'll do what I have to do."

He tugs on his beard. "If she's important to you, then she's important to me, so I'm with you all the way. We'll do our best to get her out."

Spotting a sign for The Gas Station Motel, I point to a warehouse near an older motel. A feeling of dreads sweeps over me. "There it is. I hope she's in there, like that man said, and we can get her out."

Mercury parks out front. He puts a finger to his lips. "Don't slam the door when you get out. Gently shut it, so they won't know we're coming."

"Got it." I lean over, giving him a quick kiss on the lips. "If this is the last time we see each other, I love you."

"I love you too. Now let's go get Emily."

"And her cat."

I climb out of the car, quietly shut the door and gaze at an ominous dark building, where my niece might be held.

34

FRANKIE

I place calls to other FBI agents to coordinate a search on the warehouse, while my partner Mark Brick gives local police a heads up. We hop in my car, and I barrel down the road, heading for a warehouse in the middle of nowhere.

Driving through heavy rain, I say, "These crooks were clever to put an organ harvesting operation in a rural area, surrounded by farm fields, far from prying eyes."

"I doubt we'll find the brains behind it on site. Whoever it is will be pulling strings from a distance and staying safe."

"We can only hope to catch them in the act, before harm comes to Jacklyn's niece. What'd the local cops say when you called?"

"I think I woke him up from a nap. He didn't sound

interested. Said he'd drive by and see if anything was going on."

I clear my throat. "I hope Jacklyn doesn't get there before us. I want to surprise the gang working inside, not have Jacklyn or the local cop alert them."

Brick says, "It's possible he might be on their payroll."

A silence settles over the car, and I focus on the wet, dark road. "I hope not. But you never know."

35

JACKLYN

ercury hands me a tire iron, and I put it inside my coat. Nodding to him, I set off toward the warehouse. But just as I turn the front door handle, bright lights of a squad car flash in my eyes.

The police car parks by the front door, and I freeze in place. An officer lumbers over, hitching up his pants. He's shorter than me and stout. Hopefully with this officer's help, we can get my niece out, and I'll bring her home with me to Millersville.

He flashes a badge, but I can't catch his name or badge number. Rain drums down on an overhang by the door, and he says, "May I ask what you're doing here on this dark night?"

"I'm looking for my niece. I haven't heard from her,

and I spoke with someone who told me she was here. I'm worried."

He squints and pulls down the brim of his hat. "Who told you that?"

I don't want to mention the mysterious man who answered Emily's phone, because he might get in trouble. I open my arms for emphasis, but the tire iron falls out, clanking on the ground. Ignoring my mistake, I say, "We tracked her phone here."

He frowns. "You said we. Who is the other person? Is someone with you?"

I gulp. "No, it's just me, as you can see. Only me. You're making me nervous, the way you're leaning in and staring, like something's wrong."

He looks around the parking lot. "Is that your rig there?"

"Well, yes."

"I'm going to impound it and arrest you for attempted breaking and entering, by using a tire iron."

My mouth falls open. "But that's nonsense. How would I break in with that? Besides, I'm alone on a dark night, as you said. I carry it for self-defense, and I forgot it was in my coat."

"Uh, huh. Tell that to the judge when I wake her up."

Before I can react, he handcuffs my wrists and puts me in the back of the squad car, closing the door. I rap on the window, but he doesn't look over while he makes a call on his phone. I don't see Mercury anywhere, so I hope he got away and will do something to save the day.

Leaning back against the seat, I wrinkle my nose at foul smells of urine and body odor wafting up from the upholstery.

Outside, the police officer looks down at his feet, talking into a phone. Mercury peers around a corner of the building and gives me a thumbs up sign. He surprisingly pulls a black face mask over his head and hurries away before the police officer turns and spots him.

I watch the building for signs of life and murmur to myself. "Come on, you can do it. Go get her, before it's too late."

36

FRANKIE

My partner Special Agent Mark Brick gets a call while we're underway. He answers, talks for a while and hangs up, slamming a fist into his palm. "This wasn't supposed to happen. We have to assume the worst."

I keep my eyes trained on the road. "What happened?"

"The officer I spoke with drove by the warehouse and arrested Jacklyn Stone. He says a tire iron fell out of her coat when he apprehended her at the front door. She was about to break in."

Flicking on the flashing lights, I push on the accelerator to increase our speed. It's a dark rainy evening, but I'll be careful. "We have to get there before the people inside realize what's happening and leave before we arrest them. If they're really there, that is."

He nods. "I agree."

Coming up on a tractor with blinkers on, taking up most of the road, I slow down and use the megaphone to order the farmer to the shoulder of the road. Pulling around the tractor, I speed up again and say, "Call me paranoid, but do you think that tractor was a coincidence or intentional, to stop us?"

Brick shrugs. "Could be collusion, but we may never know." He points. "There's The Gas Station Motel and the warehouse next to it. What's our plan on how we approach?"

"Given that our cover was blown by the local cop, I say we go in with all we've got. Any argument with that?"

"None from me. Shock and awe, here we come."

37

EMILY

Clutching the cat, I shuffle ahead in the dark open space. Cold air blows from an overhead fan. I stop and assess the situation. I'm not outside, like I thought I'd be. I'm in a huge warehouse, and I can't tell which way to go. I'm lost.

I say, "Hello? Is anyone there?"

Overhead lights flick on, and I flinch. My cat meows.

I squint and see Fletcher, Counter Guy, Helmet Hair, the four nurses, the old grizzled man and the gray-haired woman, who were in bed. Out of the group steps my friend Mellie, coming toward me with open arms.

I'm light-headed and confused. Is this part of the clinical trial? What's she doing here? I don't know what's happening.

Mellie brushes back strands of blond hair from her

face and frowns, saying, "They insisted I come here because you're being difficult. Can't you do just one thing right for a change?"

I cock my head, marveling at how much her words sound like my mother's when she berated me. Mellie sounds like she was part of this, but it can't be true. No friend would subject another person to this horror knowingly.

I set my cat down on the ground and grip her leash, glancing around and trying to process what's taking place. I glance at Fletcher, who wears a dark, brooding look on his face. He stares at his feet and won't meet my eyes. Something more sinister is afoot, and we won't walk off into dewy grass at sunrise, carefree and laughing. But that was never written into our story, given how he's on the other side of the law and letting them carve me up for profit, leaving me to die.

Counter Guy folds his arms, shifting from side to side. He grins with a malicious glint in his eyes. Nurses give me woeful glances, as if I'm headed for more trouble, and turn away, talking to each other. If, as I suspect, something more awful lies ahead, I'll make sure it won't happen to me. Mellie seems to be involved, although I can't figure out a connection between her and the crime ring.

Mellie grins. "I thought you'd like this game. Pretty cool, isn't it?"

My stomach knots at her betrayal. In a tight voice, I say, "I can't believe you subjected me to this. You're no friend of mine, not one bit. I almost died because of what you did. This is no prank, and I think you know that. This is deadly serious. Criminals are involved, and people die. How in the world could you risk my life?"

Her smile falters. "Oh, come on, it's not that big a deal. Everyone has two kidneys, and you can give away one. They'll pay you for it."

I step forward and slap her face. My cat hisses at her, swiping a paw. Turning to Helmet Hair, I say in a loud voice, "She can take my place, for all I care. I'll be on my way. Where are my car keys and clothes?"

Mellie points to a door.

I say, "As if I'd believe you after what you did. Nope, you can't trick me anymore. I won't trust anything you say. You go first."

Picking up my cat, I put a hand on Mellie's shoulder and shove her forward.

Mellie stops in her tracks. "No, you go on without me. I'm fine."

I propel her forward, pushing her ahead, and fling open a door. Mellie falls down a set of stairs. She screams and lands crumpled in a heap. Looking up with hair in her eyes, she says, "It wasn't supposed to be like this. They said I had to play along."

My mind is clear from whatever drug they gave me, and I scowl at my former best friend. "You should've said no and turned them into the police."

Mellie whimpers and holds her arm, which is bent at

an odd angle. "I couldn't let them hurt me, so I gave them your name. I think my arm is broken. Please, help me."

My mouth falls open. "You gave them my name? What happened? Tell me."

Tears trickle down her cheeks. "I had to pick someone, or they'd ruin me. You lost your job, and your family was dead. I figured no one would miss you."

I snort. "You decided my life wasn't worth anything, so you threw me away to protect yourself?" My mind races, reminded of the times she cancelled on me at the last minute because she had other plans. I was the last pick of her friends, and I'd moped about it, but now I understand who she really is.

She says, "I couldn't let them release nude photos from my phone to the public. They blackmailed me. I had to do it."

I jab a finger at her. "It's your fault I'm here. Screw you for saving yourself by using my life. You deserve everything that's about to happen."

I turn to the assembled group and nod to Helmet Hair. "Take Mellie and do what you like with her. Use her in your experiment and harvest her organs. Now, give me my car keys and suitcase."

Helmet Hair says to Counter Guy, Fletcher and the nurses, "We can use both of them."

They grab my betraying friend, who brought me to the brink of death.

My hands tremble, holding my cat.

Counter Guy says to me, "Move it. Let's go."

My heart races. I almost escaped, but now I'm trapped again.

Helmet Hair opens the door and shoves me inside.

38

MERCURY

A dark sedan skids to a stop in the parking lot, and two FBI agents hop out. I pull off my face mask and hurry over to them, pointing to the side door. "They're in there. I think they have another person inside from what I saw at a glance."

The FBI agents, Frankie McNalley and Mark Brick, nod and step away, conferring. Frankie makes a call on her phone, and they turn and walk toward me.

She says, "Mercury Thunder, isn't it?"

"Yes, that's my name."

"We know you're in Witness Protection and were placed in Millersville, but would you like to help us out and create a distraction?"

A smile spreads across my face. Jacklyn has no idea I'm in Witness Protection, and I have no plans to tell her, because she'd want to tell everyone she knew. And then

I'd have to pick up and move to another location, leaving Jacklyn behind.

Clearing my throat, I say, "I'd be honored. But is Jacklyn still here? I don't want her to get hurt."

Brick says, "A police officer escorted her off the premises. She's in jail."

I try to picture Jacklyn as a compliant prisoner, but an image doesn't spring to mind. The agents review their plan and soon, I'm banging on the side door, yelling for help.

A guy in his twenties wearing a white lab coat opens the door. "What's the trouble?"

"My car broke down. I need to make a call from your phone inside."

He blocks the doorway. "We don't have a phone. You need to flag someone down on the road or wait in your car until morning."

I shiver, and my teeth chatter. "It's freezing out here. Let me in."

I barge inside, pushing him aside. He runs to an alarm on the wall, pulling down a lever, and a shrieking alarm goes off. Red lights flash, bringing on a headache.

FBI agents in black burst inside, striding down the halls with weapons in their hands and fanning out. I hurry over to a young man wearing a white lab coat and khaki pants and say in a commanding voice, "Turn around and put your hands behind your back."

Snapping zip ties around his wrists, I look at his blue

embroidered name tag and say, "Well, Fletcher, how's your day going?"

He sighs and shakes his head. "Not so well. All I wanted was to publish a research paper. But it all fell apart."

I walk him down the hall toward FBI agent Frankie McNalley and say, "The lengths people will go to get published, eh?"

"Never again," he says in a soft voice.

"I don't think you'll get that chance."

"I never should've worked with this crime ring."

I nod. "You're right about that. I'd say it was a bad choice."

McNalley says, "This one for me? Thanks."

Agent Mark Brick leads a blond woman in her twenties past us in handcuffs. She says in a nasal, whining voice, "My father is wealthy. You've got to let me go. Those monsters were going to take my organs. Arrest them. I'm innocent. Take off these handcuffs."

McNalley and I lock eyes and nod to each other. I say, "Where's Emily?"

Brick says, "She's in back, crying her eyes out."

I say, "I'll go get her." I trot to the back and walk inside a sterile white room with three hospital beds, wrapping my arms around Emily. She holds her cat, and we walk out to the front.

McNalley says, "Some of the local cops may be in on

this, so we'll tread carefully. One person already agreed to testify."

Fletcher says, "Who agreed to testify? I'm innocent. I just joined to use the facility for scientific research. I had no idea what was going on behind the scenes. Keep my name out of it. If this goes public, I'll never get another job again."

McNalley tilts her head. "You're going to jail."

I cringe, thinking of the horrors of what innocents experienced. After Emily and McNalley talk, I guide Emily and her cat to my truck and drive, following McNalley and Brick to the local jail.

Jacklyn is released from a cell, and she runs into my arms, almost knocking me down. I pat her back, and my hardened brittle heart melts a bit.

Emily comes slowly around the corner. "Hi, Aunt Jacklyn."

Jacklyn's blue eyes flash open wide. "Emily, you're alive. Thank goodness."

She throws her arms around her niece, tears streaming down their cheeks. The cat jumps out of Emily's arms, and sits on the floor, sniffing the air. Emily steps back and waves her hands, exclaiming about what she experienced.

Catching Jacklyn's gaze, I nod to her. We'll keep an eye on Emily.

39

MELLIE

When an FBI agent handcuffs me, I say, "I'm innocent. I have rights. I wasn't involved in any of this."

His grip is strong, and he clenches his jaw. "Come with me. Right this way."

"My dad will set you straight. He's rich beyond what you'll ever make. I have money. You can't treat me like this."

He takes me past a female FBI agent who frowns at me. An older man with a long gray beard glares at me. I shake my shoulders, trying to free my hands. "I'm innocent."

Leading me to a patrol car, he puts me in the back and closes the door. As soon as the door slams shut, I lean back in the seat, letting tears stream down my cheeks.

I bite my lip. I hope my parents won't cut off my

allowance and tell me to get a job after this. Maybe if I tell the FBI everything I know, they'll let me go.

Blowing out a breath, I feel better having a plan to wiggle out of this mess. It's too bad Blinks was caught up in this, but I have to survive, no matter what the cost. I only hung out with her because I felt sorry for her and used her as a prop to make me look better to others. I was the girl who had a heart, everyone in town thought, because I helped a poor orphan who had lost her parents.

But the truth is, I don't have a heart. I was protecting my extended family when I invited her to live with me, because I didn't want her to sue my uncle. Frowning, I recall how she ate far too much of my food after I told her she could eat what she liked from my fridge in the house my parents bought for me.

I whoosh out a breath at how my uncle was the drunk driver who killed Emily's parents on our graduation night. After that happened, my parents and I met and came up with a dry-eyed practical plan to protect what was ours and our reputation. I would befriend poor Emily and act like her bestie. If Emily discovered it was my uncle who killed her parents and she wanted to take him to court, it my job was to mention hiring a lawyer would cost a lot, which she didn't have in her bank account.

When Emily was living with me, I flopped down on the family room couch where Emily was sitting reading a book. I offered her a glass of red wine, which she accepted, to loosen her tongue. We got to talking, and I brought up my true purpose of the conversation by saying, "Any more thoughts about taking the person to court who killed your folks in that car accident?"

Her face flushed, and she placed her wine glass down on my coffee table that cost more than she'd make in a year. It was custom made by a woodworker, and I was proud of how it looked. I handed her a coaster featuring a photo of me looking my best in a white low-cut dress. "Put a coaster under your glass, would you?"

She nodded and tucked a coaster under the glass. Everything she did was in slow motion, compared to my energetic pace, but maybe it was due to grief on her part, although it was years ago her parents passed away because of my uncle. She needed to move on and get over it. She'd mourned long enough.

Emily sighed and glanced around the room, where I'd hung framed photos of myself, posing in exotic locations I'd visited around the world on my parents' dime. I hired a professional photographer to accompany me on each trip to document my life, so I could share it with others online. My mistake was having the photographer take nude photos of me, just for fun. Unfortunately, that's what led to me being a target for the organ harvesting crime ring, when they threatened to expose private photos on my phone.

Emily sat back on the couch and sighed. "No one will tell me the name of the drunk driver, and for some reason the court records are sealed. The lawyers I contacted say their hands are tied. I've about given up finding out who did this and making them pay."

I shook my head and took a sip of red wine from a winery in Eastern Washington that produced limited amounts each year, driving up the price of each case. I'd told Emily the wine cellar was off-limits, and so far she'd obeyed my order. Swallowing the velvety, rich red wine with undertones of cherries, coffee and blackberries, I hid a smile, recalling how I encouraged the new owners of the jewelry store to lay off Emily, which led to my urging her to leave town.

I said, "That's too bad. You tried your best for your parents' sake, so maybe it's time to give up and chart a new course, live somewhere else for a change."

Emily blinked a few times. "What are you talking about? I like living here. I don't want to move."

I leaned over, patting her shoulder. "I'm serious. This is coming from a place of love, and I apologize if it comes off as harsh. But you've overstayed your welcome in my house."

She blinked back tears. "But it's only been a few months, and I can't find a job."

I nodded. "You'll have an easier time getting a job somewhere else. Make a fresh start and try something new, maybe move in with the aunt you mentioned. Where does she live?"

She sniffed, wiping her eyes. In a thick voice, she said, "Millersville, in western Washington. I've never been there, and I don't want to leave. Everything I know is here."

I squeezed her shoulder. "You're brave, deep down. You can do this. Call your aunt."

Emily's lips trembled. "But I don't want to."

I set down my wine glass and stood. Righteous anger coursed through me, remembering when my parents charged me with a grave responsibility to protect my uncle.

"Shut it down," my father said.

"Silence her," Mom told me, her dark eyes boring into mine.

Dad leaned in. "You could lose everything we've given you. This problem could financially ruin our family. If you don't take care of this, we'll be forced to take back your house and the sports car and everything else we gave you."

A shudder ran through me. I couldn't exist in my current lifestyle without their support. I depend on their monthly stipend, along with Christmas gifts of tens of thousands of dollars. I said, "Whatever you need me to do for family, I'll do it."

Staring at Emily, I put my hands on my hips and delivered an ultimatum that would make my parents proud. "You have three days to pack your things and leave. I want you out of here. It's time you stopped moping around. Go live with your aunt."

Emily coughed and looked up in shock. With tears in her eyes, she said, "You're kicking me out?"

I crossed my arms. "Yes, I've reached my limit of generosity. Go call your aunt and ask if you can live with her while you look for a job there."

She blew her nose. "But other than my aunt, I know no one in Millersville."

I sat next to her, patting her leg, picturing the crime ring that was blackmailing me. "I know just the place to stop along the way. Take the scenic route, and there's a place called The Gas Station Motel that everyone's talking about. You've got to try it. You'll love it."

Emily called her aunt, they made plans, and I said goodbye to my problems. When she drove off with her cat, I grinned, because I'd solved two problems with her exit. She'd never learn my uncle was the one who caused the car crash, and she'd be an organ donor, taking my place.

Now, I purse my lips in the back seat of a squad car, recalling how I encouraged my uncle, who was an agent to sports stars, to stop by my catered party at the country club and celebrate high school graduation with my friends, drinking champagne my parents purchased by the case. Emily wasn't invited to the party, because as a pariah, she would've been a blight on the event. I didn't want a drab loser dampening the vibe of my high school graduation celebration. The party was all about me, not her.

Squirming in the back seat, I suppose I should feel a

little guilty that my uncle killed her parents that night, but I don't. My uncle survived, and her parents were in the wrong place when he ran a red light. It turned out he'd stopped at a bar for a few drinks after leaving my party, and his blood alcohol level was well above the legal limit. My family closes ranks when bad things happen, and we protect our own.

I tug at handcuffs cutting into my wrists. Things look bleak for me, but my family will pay for a top-notch lawyer, and I'll finagle my way out of jail. My parents' money makes me untouchable.

40

HELMET HAIR

An alarm goes off, and I check the exits, but they're blocked. I run to a bathroom and shut the door. Staring in the mirror, I shake my head at how I've become a middle-aged dowdy woman with dull brown hair. My alliance with a crime ring cost me plenty.

A police officer in blue barges in and handcuffs me, reading me my rights. As he leads me to a patrol car, I say, "I'm innocent."

I slide into the back of a patrol car. I won't cry for what I've lost. I'll get even. Someone called the cops, and I'll find out who snitched.

41

FRANKIE

Jacklyn and her niece throw their arms around each other in a joyous reunion, weeping and laughing. I wipe a tear from my eye and clap my hands. "Let's get started. Brick, why don't you interview Emily? I'll speak with Jacklyn briefly before I talk to the others."

Hours later, the sun is rising, and I rub my weary eyes. I love my line of work, stopping hardened criminals. But this case makes my stomach hurt, thinking about innocent lives lost and missing people who will never turn up because of a ring of organ harvesters.

Driving back to Seattle with Special Agent Brick, I say, "Interesting that the police officer on night duty was paid to keep quiet. We were lucky to catch them before they fled the area."

"Yep, they were about to cut into that blond girl. She

mentioned something about a game. We'll have to look into that angle. Do you think they lured people there by pretending it was a locked room puzzle?"

"Sounds like it," I say, blinking to keep my eyes open. "Except it was a puzzle no one could solve. Death was the only way out."

"They're blaming each other, but I think the ring leader is the woman with shoulder length brown hair. The others said she was in charge."

"I think so too, but we need to look closer at the guy who worked at the motel. I suspect he was running the operation, and he has connections to organized crime."

Bricks yawns. "Even out in the boonies, criminals hide."

I half-smile. "Or don't, in this case. Good work, Brick. It was a long night."

He grins and shrugs. "The day is just getting started."

"And we love our jobs."

42

IRENA

I wake up the next morning on Tex's couch on Grand Island. Birds chirp, and frogs croak. An aroma of fresh brewed coffee wafts past, and I sit up, stretching my arms. Kelly brings over a mug of coffee, setting it down on a live edge coffee table.

She says, "How did you sleep?"

"Pretty well. It's beautiful here, I can see why you like it."

She smiles. "Do you want to go to school with me and see my teacher?"

I point a finger at her. "Yes, and I want to speak with the boy who you rode dirt bikes with and tell him I forbid you to do that for at least three more years."

Kelly rolls her eyes. "Please, Mom, don't do that."

I lean back and sip coffee, taking in the day. It's quiet here. I haven't ever considered moving to this island, away from the hustle and bustle of town, but right now, it's an appealing idea.

Kelly says, "What are you thinking about?"

"How I understand why you like it here. I might want to live here one day."

She jumps up and claps her hands.

I stand, take the mug to the kitchen sink and rinse it out. "But I'll have to think about it."

She groans. "You always say that."

I open my arms and give her a hug. "But this time, I mean it."

Stepping back, I say, "You were lucky you weren't injured."

She nods, studying the floor. "I know, and I'm sorry I didn't listen to what you said. I'll do better next time."

I poke her arm gently with a finger. "And the time after that, and the one after that."

Tex comes in the kitchen, and she looks at us. "You two are getting along, I see."

"Yep, we'll have smooth sailing." My phone rings, and I answer it. A boater in distress needs my help. I wave to Kelly and Tex. "Thanks for letting me crash and the coffee. I've got to run."

I head for the door. "Kelly, remember to call your dad and Abby. They miss you."

"Wait, you said you'd hang out and go to school with me."

"Sorry, hon, but a boater needs me. Thanks, Tex. Love you, Kels. See you later."

I step out into the winter wind and stride to my boat, taking another call. "I'll be right there," I say and hop in my boat, grinning and starting the engine. This is my calling, and I'm lucky to love my line of work.

43

KELLY

Standing at the window, I watch my mom hurry to her boat and say to Tex, "She promised she'd go to school with me today."

"Something came up, and she has to go to work."

"I wish she worked less. The boaters come first, and I'm last in line."

Tex says, "We're coming up with ways to fix that. Just try to be patient."

I cross my arms and watch Mom's boat glide away from the dock, heading toward a boat in distress. Deep in my heart, I doubt Mom will cut back on her work schedule. She's addicted to the adrenaline rush of running to the rescue.

Letting out a sigh, I say, "I'll try."

44

EMILY

Snuggled in a quilt on my aunt's couch, I pet my cat, who is snuggled up beside me. Aunt Jacklyn's dog, who does like cats, sits on the floor with his tongue hanging out of his mouth, looking goofy.

My aunt looks up from her laptop. She sits in her favorite yellow armchair, drinking black coffee. "How's the job search going?"

I shrug. "Just fine. I have two interviews this afternoon."

She beams and leans forward. "Tell me more."

"Not yet, I don't want to jinx it. I'll tell you afterwards. But something else came up this morning. A TV station called and they want an interview, but I'd rather you did it."

She chuckles. "You know what happened, and you'd be much better on camera. What viewers would want to see me, old aunt Jacklyn hobbling along? They'd rather watch youthful, vibrant Emily, with her whole life ahead of her."

I laugh. "But I don't want to do the interview, and I suggested they ask you. You could mention your tiny home project and bring up the topic somehow."

She purses her lips. "I like that idea. I'll think it over, thanks. Maybe I'll do the interview after all."

45

DUSTY

I roll my wheelchair into the dayroom and glance at the television. To my horror, my mother is featured on a news segment about stopping an organ harvesting crime ring and how she helped break it open by calling the FBI. Her blue eyes and rosy cheeks and lantern jaw are larger than life, and I suppress a groan. I don't need reminders of my mother on television, because her presence lives large in my mind most of the time.

An aide comes in the dayroom and turns up the volume. She says, "Isn't that woman courageous? She went and tracked down her niece and got arrested by a crooked police officer, but the FBI sorted it out and her niece escaped. Jacklyn Stone is a hero in my book."

Without thinking, I rise up out of the wheelchair and grab a man's plate, throwing it with all my might at the television. The screen cracks and goes dark, and the television becomes silent. Take that, Mother, dear. I finally shut you up.

Nurse Wright rushes over and says in a stern voice, "Dusty Stone, what have you done? We'll have to replace the television a second time because of your temper, and I'll report it to your mother. She won't be pleased. You must control your temper, before we'll consider releasing you. If you don't do that, you'll become a long-term Shore Lodge resident in this ward and considered a danger to others."

I bite my tongue and suppress seething, guttural sounds. One day, I'll get out of here, but for now, it's only a dream, and life begins on the other side of Cedar Channel.

46

NATHAN FLETCHER

Sitting in a dim room in a boarding house in South Dakota, I tap a pen on the table. I'd like to write a letter to Emily Workman, but I know that isn't wise. I'm in Witness Protection, and I need to keep a low profile, so no one from my past can find me.

I crumple up a letter and toss it in the waste basket, making it the tenth time I've done this. Given our traumatic experience together in the clinic, I felt Emily and I had a tenuous bond. Letting out a sigh, I stand and make my way out of my rented room, heading to my job at the front desk of a motel in a small town.

47

JACKLYN

Emily walks in the door, and I zip up my coat. "I'm taking Buddy for a walk. Want to go?"

She grins. "No, I can't, because I'm starting a new job this afternoon."

I leash up Buddy and smile at her. "Already? Congratulations. Where will you be working? In a store downtown?"

She sways from side to side. "I'm going to work for a boat broker, detailing, buffing and polishing them. I'm really excited about it."

"That's wonderful. I'm so glad you found a job you like." I give her a hug and walk out the door, calling, "Remember to lock up when you leave."

She waves. "I will. Don't worry."

Walking away in winter wind and pelting rain, I shake my head at how Emily's mother, my sister, enjoyed complaining about her offspring. Her daughter is a delight, and nothing like what my sister described. What kind of mother leaves her daughter at home alone on her high school graduation night to go off and eat dinner out with her husband?

I shrug. I shouldn't judge, because I have no idea what really went on in that house. But I'll do my best to protect my niece from harm for the rest of my life.

A pickup truck parks by the curb, and Mercury climbs out. "Thought I might find you out here. Care for some company?"

I smile. "Buddy and I would love it."

My dog rubs his eyes, wet from the rain, on the leg of Mercury's jeans, and Mercury pats his head. "Kind of wet out here for us old guys, isn't it, Buddy?"

My dog pants and smiles. A squirrel scampers up a nearby tree, and Buddy stops to stare. I say, "I know that twitching tail is distracting, but you'd better leave it until you can climb trees."

We march through the rain, and Mercury and I link arms. I smile to myself and watch Buddy sniff blades of wet grass.

Mercury's voice breaks into my thoughts. "Any news about your tiny home project?"

Rain drops hit my eyes, and I blink. "Yes, it looks like we can fit eighty tiny homes on the parcel, according to the engineer, but we're planning forty to start. I can add more later. Calls came in from my television interviews, and lots of people put down deposits. I'm all set, and I don't need an outside investor."

He says, "That's too bad, because I was going to offer you my two cents."

We burst out laughing and continue on our way, and I tell him about Emily's job offer. He says, "Anyone who likes to clean boats will have a job for life in this town. That's extremely good news."

We turn the corner and head for home, but a large sturdy buck with antlers blocks our way. A musky smell comes off the big beast, and I wrinkle my nose. "We're not tangling with him," I say. "Let's let him have the right of way."

Later at home, snug by a blazing fire, I pat Buddy dry with a towel and brush his fur.

"He's a lucky dog," Mercury says.

I smile. "We're both lucky."

Emily's cat meows from her crate in the guest bedroom, which was Dusty's room growing up. Buddy pricks his ears and sits up, but I pat his back. "Leave it. Mint Julep is a sweet girl. She's family now."

My dog settles down with a groan, and the fire crackles, warming me. I have a feeling we're in for a bright future, if we can survive the winter storms.

48

EMILY

I've learned how to buff and polish boat hulls, chrome and brass. When I'm finished with each job, I step back with a smile and a sense of pride. Crossing my arms, I survey my latest accomplishment and nod, but wince when I think of my former friend Mellie. She pretended to be my friend and deceived me, while working behind my back.

During interviews with the FBI, Mellie blamed her involvement on me. Fortunately, the FBI believed me, not her, and not her rich parents' lawyers. I'm free, while Mellie is in jail. Talk about a turn-around, where justice is served.

I grin. I can't wait to tell Aunt Jacklyn and Mint Julep about my excellent day working on boats at the marina. I'm saving up to rent a place of my own, but I've found a new home in Millersville. I'm learning what family should be about.

49

KARINA

I hurry to the front counter and prepare a secret take-out order for Jacklyn and her niece, who just moved to town. With a smile, I slide two pieces of warm quiche into containers and plop two scones into white paper sacks. I say to my assistant, Bernard Frackus, "They'll be surprised when you hand them these. They'll be delighted."

I scribble down on a piece of paper, 'Welcome to town! Love, Karina and Bernard.'

He fiddles with his glasses. "But it's free? Why are we doing this?"

I slip the note in the sack with the scones. The mouth-watering aroma of bacon wafts out of the quiche container. "It's our welcome to Millersville gift, to make Emily feel special. Okay, go now and take it over there while it's hot."

He nods. "Understood. I'll be right back."

"Stay as long as you like. We're in a lull, and I'll be fine."

He picks up the containers and marches out the door, heading into the wind and rain with a determined look, like the high school science teacher he once was.

I pick up a coffee pot and breeze around the restaurant, located on the lower floor of my old two-story home, refilling cups. A woman in a pink sweatshirt and sweatpants flags me down and says in a low voice, "Did you hear what happened? Jacklyn Stone's niece moved to town. I heard she had a run in with a crime ring at a motel a few hours from here. Is what we saw on the news true?"

I suppress a chuckle, because gossip is the coin of trade in my hometown. I moved away to Seattle to work as an artist, and I was content in the city until my ailing grandmother pulled me back and made me promise to run Gigi's Café after she passed away. My deathbed promise changed my life, and I went from a carefree artist to a homeowner and a business person in the blink of an eye, when Gigi died.

Nodding, I say, "Yes, I heard that happened. We're lucky she lived to tell the tale."

Her fellow book club member taps a hand on a paperback book on the table. "I knew the news reports were right, and Jacklyn Stone was involved. We'll have to suggest she write a book about her story. I'd read it."

Ms. Pink says, "I would too."

I move on to other tables and cash customers out. Ever since Jacklyn was on the news, strangers have been coming to town, all abuzz about the heroines in Millersville. Stacking dirty plates in a plastic tray and carrying them to the kitchen in back, where my grand-mother was queen of scones and quiches, teaching me everything I knew and raising me, I nod to myself. In Millersville, we're all heroes and heroines, with our own secret stories to tell.

I stride back to the front of the café and bid people goodbye, closing the door behind them and shutting out the howling wind and cascade of dried leaves tumbling inside. The door opens, and I turn, breaking into a wide smile and opening my arms, hugging the woman I didn't know was my half-sister, even though we both lived in the same town.

Gesturing to a table, I say to Violet, "Sit, and I'll get you a cup of coffee. Would you like a slice of bacon cheese quiche and a scone?"

She grins. "Yes, if you have some left. I'm famished."

A warm feeling spreads across my chest, as a wave of gratefulness sweeps over me for having the sister I'd always wanted. Holding up an index finger, I say, "I'll get your food, and we'll catch up. Be right back."

She goes over and pours herself a steaming mug of coffee. "I'm family, so no need to serve me."

Soon, we're seated at a two-top, laughing about our pathetic attempts at dating. She nibbles on a scone and groans at the flavor my grandmother taught me to infuse into each item we baked. When her plate is clean, she pushes it aside and looks me in the eyes. "You won't believe what I've been up to."

"I want to hear all about it."

50

JACKLYN

Someone knocks at the door, and I look out to see my neighbor, Bernard Frackus standing outside with two bags in his hands. Wondering what he's doing here, I open the door, gesturing for him to come inside.

"Hello, Bernard. Come in. Get out of the wind and rain."

Wind howls down the street, gusting at twenty-five miles an hour. Bernard steps inside and shivers. My dog Buddy stretches and comes over, sniffing the white sacks.

Bernard says, "These are welcome to town gifts from Gigi's Café for your niece and you to share."

I call, "Emily, come out. You have a present from Gigi's Café."

Emily comes out of her room and a smile spreads across her face. "A gift? For me?"

Bernard beams and hands her the bags. "These are for you from the café, from Karina and me. Better eat them while they're hot. The scones are the best I've ever had. Karina's grandmother came up with the recipe."

I pat his shoulder. "I know you miss Gigi. I'm sorry for your loss."

He wipes his eyes. "You never get over it. But we go on with our lives, don't we? Working at Gigi's Café keeps me busy and lets me feel close to her."

"I'm glad you're doing that and helping Karina. She says great things about you. Care to join us for a cup of coffee?"

He shrugs. "I'm kind of coffeed-out for the day, but I could stop for a quick chat while you two eat. I'm not needed at the café for a while."

We sit in the kitchen at the round table and tell stories. Emily takes a bite of a scone, and her eyes grow wide. Brushing crumbs from her mouth, she says, "This is really good. I'm glad to know about this place, because I'll be over there all the time."

When the quiche is gone and the scones have been reduced to mere crumbs, Bernard stands. "I'd best be on my way. Time to get back."

Emily and I rise, and she makes me proud when she says, "Please tell Karina thank you. I really appreciate the gesture. I'm so glad I moved here to be near my aunt."

He walks out the door, into howling wind and driving cold rain, and hurries to his car. I turn to Emily and say,

"That was one of my wonderful neighbors, and he lives right across the street. I'm very fortunate to live here."

Emily hugs me. "And I'm lucky to be joining you. Thanks for inviting me. But I want you to know, I'm saving up to rent my own place."

Buddy nuzzles the cat, who swats him, and he leaps back.

"No rush," I say, "but it might be best at some point to separate our pets."

51

FRANKIE

onths later, I slap high fives with Special Agent Mark Brick. "We've got the crime ring locked up behind bars for good. Way to go partner."

He frowns. "I wish we would've kept track of that guy who worked at the motel front desk, but we don't know where he is. He might've left for Mexico after he squealed on his accomplices."

"He'll surface soon enough, and we'll be watching for him. It helped that the researcher at the university cooperated. He's in witness protection. Do you think Jacklyn's niece Emily is safe, with the counter guy at large? If she's in danger, we should we warn her."

Brick rubs his chin. "I'd say she's fine, and let's not bother her. She's been through so much. She's safe for now."

52

COUNTER GUY

I stare into Jacklyn Stone's house, watching for her niece to make an appearance, but all I see is a beagle-mix dog. I grit my teeth and vow once again to get back at the young woman who kicked up trouble, leading to my financial ruin. When the Feds cracked down on our crime ring, I lost my job. I offered to make a deal with the Feds and slithered out of doing more jail time. When I got out, I went off the grid and got a disguise.

I smile, envisioning taking Emily out of town and removing her kidneys and her liver. A deal like that will bring in mega bucks and could kill her.

Rubbing my hands together, I review my plan. I hired a physician who is down on his luck from gambling debts, and I set up an operating room in a warehouse. I've found buyers on the dark web, and I'll assist during the operation, delivering organs and disposing of the donor's body. Check, check and check, for having handled those tasks in the past. By the time the aunt squawks, if she does, I'll have moved on to a new location, where no one will find me.

Glancing in the rear-view mirror, I nod to myself. I shaved my thinning hair, grew a mustache, and I'm wearing fake bifocals as a disguise. A black watch cap and black sweat pants and a sweatshirt give me a younger vibe, like I'm an athletic type and not a dud who stands behind a motel front desk all day. I doubt Emily will recognize me when I go up to her and talk her into helping me by getting in to my car and showing me where a distant park on the water is located.

My body stills when Emily walks outside and gets in her car. She drives away, and I follow her, humming a happy tune. Scores of people want organs, and there aren't enough to go around. If organ donation was the default on driver's licenses, it might make a dent in my profits, but I'll be in business, preying on vulnerable people for a long time.

Driving through a small waterfront town, I follow Emily to the marina and pull over, watching her hop out of her car. She fiddles with her purse before striding into an office, and I bite my tongue, biding my time. I'll grab her after she finishes work, when she'll be distracted and exhausted.

53

EMILY

I hurry around a corner and hide by the Border Patrol and U.S. Customs Office in Millersville at the marina. Dialing my aunt, I say when she picks up, "That guy I told you about?"

Aunt Jacklyn says, "Yes, did you see him again?"

"Yeah, the guy from the motel front counter followed me from your house to the marina parking lot. He's wearing a black knit cap and dark sweatpants and a sweatshirt. He's driving a white SUV with Washington plates. He's wearing glasses this time and it looks like he might've shaved his head."

"Stay somewhere safe and don't work on a boat by yourself. I'll call Special Agent McNalley and tell her we found him."

I hang up and stride into the Customs Office, reading notices on a bulletin board while keeping an eye on the parking lot. I text my boss to say I'm running late and say I'll explain why later. She texts back, 'K.'

I smile, feeling lucky to have landed a job working mostly by myself and polishing things until the sun makes them shine. I'm looking forward to spending my summer near the San Juan Islands. Maybe I'll take up kayaking, but my aunt isn't a fan of that, mentioning strong currents, which can become dangerous.

I swallow hard. The Counter Guy is parked in the lot, looking at his phone. At the sound of sirens coming closer, he looks up, and meets my gaze through the window. My stomach knots, and I silently urge the FBI to get here fast and haul this horrible person away to prison.

He drives out of the parking lot, but two sedans block him in, screeching to a halt. His car is boxed in, and Counter Guy jumps out and runs toward a hot dog shop. I hope no bystanders will be in the tiny store at this early hour, because Counter Guy has no moral compass. He's hurt innocent people to get his way in the past, and he'll do it again with no regrets. It's all about money to him.

A woman in a blue jacket runs after Counter Guy, leaping ahead and bringing him down. I can't help but jump up and down, clapping my hands at the sight of one of my tormenters led away in handcuffs.

Blowing out a breath, I smile. Now I'm finally safe. I ripped a letter from Nathan Fletcher to shreds last night, after taking a photo of it and sending it to Agent McNalley and showing it to my aunt.

A Customs agent stands up from his desk and asks, "Is there anything we can help you with?"

I grin and gesture to the window. "No, thanks. It looks like the FBI solved my problems."

As the FBI agents drive away, the Customs and Border Patrol agents go back to their desks. I wave goodbye and hurry out the door to the boat broker's office.

My boss stands and points outside. "Did you see that? They caught a guy in the parking lot. Did you hear what was going on?"

I nod. "Yeah, that's why I was late. He was following me, and my aunt contacted the FBI. It's a long story that started at a motel in the middle of nowhere. I'll tell you about it sometime over coffee or a beer."

She adjusts her frizzy blond hair pulled up in a bun and beams. "Let's go to the Brown after work and you can tell me about it."

Later, at The Brown Lantern, we sit side by side on bar stools. Bets, a bartender, comes over. "What'll you have? Do you know what you'd like yet?"

I point to a bright yellow warning sign stuck on the edge of the counter. "What's that drink like? It's called Danger Signs?"

She smiles. "I'll bring you a taste, so you can see what it's like. It's really for bartenders, though, because not many people like it."

I grin and look at Retta, my boss. "I've tasted danger before, so I'll try it."

A man with a dragon tattoo on his neck comes out of the back, saying to Bets, "Have you seen my gold nail clippers? I can't find them."

"Hon," Bets says, cocking her head, "we'll find them later. I can't be the only one serving people in this after-work rush." Bets points to me. "Give her a sample of Danger Signs and take their order."

He sets down a shot glass with a murky brown liquid in front of me. "See what you think. Only a few of us like it, to be honest."

Taking a sip, I swallow, tasting bitterness with a pleasant aftertaste. I set it down and wrinkle my nose. "Thanks, but I've had enough danger lately. I'll have a vodka martini."

He slaps the bar top with a meaty hand. "Got it. And for you?"

Retta says, "I'll have the same, thanks. Emily, give me a taste of that danger stuff. I could use a little zip in my life."

We laugh, and Zerk turns away, Bets bustles behind the bar, and I release a sigh. Everything is going to fine after all. I'm safe.

I slide the shot glass of the dark brown liquid over to her. My phone buzzes with a text from my aunt, saying, 'What happened at the marina? Everything OK?'

Glancing at my phone, I say to Retta, "Sorry, but my aunt is really important to me. I'll text her back and put this away."

I text Aunt Jacklyn, 'All good. They hauled him away. I'm safe.'

She texts, 'Phew. When are you coming home?'

'I'm at the Brown. Not sure when I'll be home.'

'Have a French 75 for me. See u later.'

Retta says as I pocket my phone, "You're close with your aunt. I envy that."

I shrug. "She's my only living relative, and I'm lucky to be related to her."

She sips the syrupy thick brown drink from the shot glass and coughs, clapping a hand over her chest. "Gak, what is this?"

I grin. "It's full of danger with a strange aftertaste that I liked, but not enough to drink more of it."

Retta sets the shot glass down on the bar with a thump. She leans in. "Tell me what happened at the marina today and why you were late."

"Here's what happened. Do you want me to start from the beginning?"

"Of course."

"Well, it all started with my friend Mellie. She sent me to The Gas Station Motel, which turned out to be linked to an organ harvesting crime ring."

Retta claps a hand to her mouth. "I heard about that. Tell me more."

I continue with the story, and soon Bets and Zerk are drawn to us, hovering on the other side of the bar, exclaiming at events that unfolded. Bar patrons gather round, listening. When I'm through with my tale, the bar crowd gives me a standing ovation.

My face heats, and I smile. This is what it's like to be seen and appreciated for who I am, and I'm discovering I like it.

Don't miss out on news about my books! Subscribe to my author newsletter on my website: www. susanspechtoram.com

Thank you for reading *The Gas Station Motel*! Please let other readers know what to expect by posting ratings and reviews on Goodreads, Amazon and BookBub.

Jacklyn's story begins in *Shore Lodge* and continues in *The Winter Storm, The Cold Night, Avalanche* and *These Lies*

Irena's story begins in *Under Jackson Bridge,* and continues in *Missing Man* and *By Midnight*

Karina's story begins in *Secrets at the Café*

Violet's story begins in *Cabin Eight* and continues in *The Mother's Threat*

Bets and Zerk first appear in *The Thieves*

Like a short thrilling read? *A Chilling Christmas Eve* is a story of greed and murderous intentions.

Francesca and her brother thought they'd be rich. But when their estranged father dies without a will, their wealthy grandmother leaves her estate to the gardener. Francesca flies to California to change her grandmother's mind and get the money she deserves. But the gardener has other plans...
Read *A Chilling Christmas Eve!*

THANK YOU

Follow me on BookBub for updates

Follow me on my Facebook author page

If you're on YouTube, check out my channel for audiobooks and nature photography @susanspechtoramauthor

Thank you for reading my books!

ABOUT THE AUTHOR

Susan is writing mysteries-thrillers and creative nonfiction. Previously, she served as senior director of corporate communications for biotechnology companies. Susan worked as an activity aide in an upscale nursing home's secure psychiatric unit. She was a potter and painter with an art studio in Seattle and has also worked as a market researcher, a nurse's aide, a waitress, and a library page. Her essays have been published in Mothering Magazine, Twins Magazine and Utne Reader. Susan grew up near Detroit, Michigan. She lives in a windy part of the Pacific Northwest with her husband and rescue dog.

Mysteries-Thrillers
  Shore Lodge
  The Thieves
  Cabin Eight
  Secrets at the Café
  The Mother's Threat
  Under Jackson Bridge
  Missing Man
  By Midnight

The Winter Storm

The Cold Night

Avalanche

These Lies

The Gas Station Motel

A Chilling Christmas Eve

Creative Nonfiction: Strangers on a Train Series

Green Light

The Train

Canoe

Soup Kettle

Bathtub

Phone Call

Watering Can

Waterfall

Strangers on a Train Series collection (Books 1-8) (available in ebook, paperback and hard cover)

Humorous fiction:

Boating with Buddy, a report from a canine correspondent

Nonfiction:

Brief business books on investor relations, crisis communication and public relations